PHANTOM

FLEET

Secrets Beneath the Waves

ECHO SABLE

Table of Contents

Chapter 1

Ghost Ship on the Sea

The annals of maritime history are filled with tales of tragedy, yet few are as indelibly etched into the collective consciousness as the Titanic's — a colossal symbol of human ambition, brought low by an iceberg on its maiden voyage.

But even before the Titanic's infamous night, the sea claimed countless other vessels. The past, often shrouded in mystery and lacking detailed records, tells of the Mongolian fleet, an armada swallowed by a hurricane as it set sail to conquer Japan. This saga of ambition and devastation, nearly forgotten amidst the tides of time, remains a whisper in history's vast expanse.

These fragmented and elusive stories remind us of the ocean's might and mystery—a force shaping human history through triumph and tragedy. They serve as a testament to the sea's enduring allure and peril, and the countless narratives hidden beneath its waves.

The Titanic's demise, however, occurred in an era of burgeoning communication, its tragedy instantly reverberating across the globe. Stories of its sinking transcended reality, inspiring novels and cinema, embedding deeply into the human psyche—a shipwreck known to every soul.

In modern television, a daring American company has blurred the lines between fiction and history, creating a science fiction series that manipulates time itself. One particularly gripping episode revolves around the Titanic's fateful encounter with an iceberg—a moment poised for temporal interference.

Two intrepid travelers from our era find themselves inexplicably cast back across decades, suddenly aboard a grand passenger liner. As the awe-inspiring reality dawns, they recognize with horror that they are aboard the RMS Titanic, the ill-fated ship destined for disaster.

Armed with knowledge from the future, the duo urgently seeks out the ship's captain—a seasoned mariner tempered by a lifetime at sea, yet bound by the chains of skepticism. They fervently warn him of the looming icy catastrophe. But their impassioned pleas are met with incredulity, perceived as the ravings of lunatics. In response, they are detained, their voices of reason swallowed by the ship's bustling corridors, their dire warnings echoing unheard amidst the cacophony of impending doom.

And yet, history's relentless march could not be thwarted. The Titanic collided with its iceberg, the tragedy unfolding as it always had.

As I delve into this tale, an intriguing concept unfolds—a story I would write with a slight alteration. Imagine if two modern-day travelers, armed with foreknowledge, approach the Titanic's captain. Initially, he dismisses their warnings, but as doubt gnaws at him, he eventually decides to change the ship's course, hoping to sidestep disaster.

Yet, despite these efforts, the Titanic still meets its fateful end, colliding with an iceberg just as history records.

My inclination to alter the tale is rooted in the enigmatic aura surrounding the Titanic's tragedy.

From the outset, the disaster has been wrapped in mystery.

For starters, the presence of massive icebergs along the Titanic's route defied expectations—such obstacles should not have existed. Moreover, the ship was equipped with state-of-the-art technology for its time, capable of detecting and avoiding icebergs. Yet, despite these advantages, the Titanic met its catastrophic fate, as though guided by an unseen hand.

The discovery of the Titanic's wreck in 1985 added a compelling chapter to its storied history. The cameras aboard the exploring submarine captured haunting images of the ship's vast interior and exterior, giving the world a glimpse into the remains of what was once a symbol of human ambition and engineering prowess. Yet, the absence of the thousands of victims' bodies introduced another layer of mystery to the already enigmatic tragedy, fueling speculation and intrigue.

Despite its resting place on the ocean floor being pinpointed, the question of when, or even if, the Titanic could ever be fully salvaged remains unanswered. The logistical challenges and ethical considerations surrounding such an endeavor are significant. Nonetheless, the Titanic continues to reign as the preeminent shipwreck, capturing imaginations and standing as an enduring symbol of both human achievement and vulnerability. Its story, rich with lessons and emotions, remains firmly anchored in the collective consciousness, ensuring its place as the protagonist among maritime disasters.

On June 18, 2023, a sightseeing submarine exploring the Titanic wreckage lost contact just 1 hour and 45 minutes after its morning departure, casting a somber and mysterious shadow over the site of the infamous shipwreck.

Among the five aboard was British billionaire Hamish Harding.

By June 22, 2023, the U.S. Coast Guard confirmed that the submarine had imploded near the Titanic's resting place, tragically claiming the lives of all five passengers. Alongside Hamish Harding were Stockton Rush, president of Oceangate — the company operating the submarine—and Paul-Henry, a skilled French submarine pilot.

The cause of this devastating accident remains undetermined, adding a new layer of mystery to the already haunting legacy of the Titanic.

My tale, aptly titled "Phantom Fleet," plunges into the enigmatic depths of maritime disaster, steering clear of time travel and the Titanic's story. Yet, the Titanic serves as a poignant prologue—a reminder that "absolute safety" is but an illusion on the capricious sea. The unsinkable Titanic met its doom on its maiden voyage, a testament to the unpredictable and mysterious nature of the ocean.

In our modern age, advancements in science and technology have endowed ships with sophisticated safety measures. One might think such progress would shield vessels from calamity. However, consider the U.S. nuclear-powered submarine Thresher, which vanished into the abyss of the Atlantic Ocean, its loss shrouded in mystery. What greater testament to the sea's unpredictability?

Despite the ocean's capricious nature, humanity's fervor for exploration remains undiminished. For thousands of years, we've been drawn to the sea's vastness, undeterred by its mysteries. Shipwrecks, once sensational events, now occur with such regularity that they scarcely make headlines. Yet, each one serves as a somber reminder of the ocean's formidable power—a force that continues to captivate and challenge us, even as it humbles our aspirations.

A friend, cryptic in his invitation, led me to this tale. He spoke of Captain Moore, a man with whispers of the sea's secrets to share.

Our meeting unfolded in the dim ambiance of a bar— a place where stories, like the tides, ebb and flow.

In my mind's eye, a captain is a figure of gravitas—a middle-aged man with a commanding beard, tall and dignified, clad in a crisp uniform adorned with gold-trimmed cuffs and collar. A presence that commands attention.

Yet, as I entered the bar, the man who approached was a stark contrast to my imagination. He was young, perhaps twenty-seven or twenty-eight, with a dark complexion and a slender build. His movements were quick and assured, his attire casual and unassuming.

His face was open and friendly, eyes bright with intelligence. As soon as he spotted me, he extended a hand in greeting. "You must be Mr. Morris. I'm Moore."

Surprised, I replied, "Oh, Captain Moore?"

He nodded, shaking my hand with genuine warmth. "It's a pleasure to finally meet you. My mother is Maori Native, and truth be told, my best skill is actually canoeing!"

His candor drew a laugh from me, immediately putting me at ease. There was an unaffected charm about Moore—a refreshing absence of pretense. We settled into our seats, ready to dive into the conversation that awaited us.

His lively and straightforward demeanor suggested there was no need for formalities. So I got to the point. "Captain, my friend mentioned you have a challenging matter to discuss with me. I'm flattered you would seek my counsel."

Moore chuckled, revealing a neat set of white teeth, likely a trait inherited from his Maori heritage. "First off, don't call me 'Captain.' That's just my profession. If we go by titles, I'd have to call you 'Chairman of the Import and Export Company, Adventurer, and Writer!'"

I laughed along, feeling an immediate connection with him. "Alright, Moore, you seem to know quite a bit about me. So, what is it you'd like to discuss?"

Moore's expression shifted, his smile fading into a look of earnestness. After a pause that felt laden with meaning, he spoke. "I should start by introducing myself properly, so you don't dismiss my words as the wild tales of a Maori native."

I gestured with open hands, signaling my interest. "By all means, go ahead."

Captain Moore began, "My mother is a humble Maori woman, and she's never had the chance for formal education. My father, on the other hand, comes from a very affluent background, which is why I received the same education as any white child. Perhaps it's my Maori heritage that draws me to the sea. After a year of studying literature in college, I realized my true passion lay elsewhere and shifted my focus to sailing."

I nodded, understandingly. "Anyone with a heart for adventure rarely sticks to literature, even if they dream of writing someday."

Moore chuckled. "After I graduated from navigation school, the sea became my home. I became a captain a year ago, and I assure you, it was my skill that earned me that position, not my father's stake in the shipping company."

"I've no doubt about your abilities," I replied with a smile.

His face lit up at my words, but then a shadow crossed his features as he sighed, "But now, I have no ship."

I raised an eyebrow, and he offered a wry smile. "My ship sank, and the incident is under investigation. Until it's resolved, I'm left without a vessel. If they find the sinking was my fault—" He paused, his voice dropping to a hoarse whisper, "I may never command a ship again."

His words struck a chord, and I felt a pang of sympathy. It was clear how deeply he cherished his life at sea. The prospect of losing that seemed devastating.

For a moment, I was at a loss for words. The sinking of a ship can happen for myriad reasons, and from what he said, it appeared he might be bearing the brunt of the blame.

Moore's demeanor was somber as he lowered his head. After a pause, he reached into his briefcase, producing a map. He unfolded it, pointing to a spot. "This is where the shipwreck occurred."

I glanced at the location he indicated and recognized it as a part of the Atlantic Ocean near Bermuda—a place notorious for its mysteries.

Bermuda Island, perched in the vast expanse of the Atlantic, stands isolated like a lone sentinel. Its geography is nothing short of extraordinary. A glance at any map reveals its solitary nature—the West Indies lie over a thousand kilometers to the south, and to the north, the distance is equally daunting. To the west, the situation becomes even bleaker, as one must traverse nearly the length of the American continent before encountering another island.

In essence, Bermuda is surrounded by a thousand-kilometer void, devoid of any significant landmasses. Historically, navigators have regarded the journey to Bermuda as perilous. Sailors of old would often say, "Spend enough time at sea, and you'll encounter all manner of oddities."

When Moore indicated a spot approximately 100 kilometers south of Bermuda, I was taken aback.

"I have friends in the seafaring community who refer to this region as the Devil's Triangle," I mentioned. "It's notoriously treacherous for sailors."

Moore nodded, a bitter smile on his lips. "It was in this very area that my ship went down."

His voice carried a weight of sorrow as he recounted the shipwreck, seemingly oblivious to my interjection. "My vessel was a medium-sized cargo ship, equipped with advanced technology and manned by a crew of 26."

As he spoke, his voice grew raspier, laden with the burden of loss.

It was then that Moore looked me in the eye and revealed the full extent of the tragedy. "All twenty-six crew members... none survived."

Moore's hands gripped the map, fists clenched so tightly that I could hear the joints cracking.

I reached over, gently placing my hand over his. "Sometimes, disasters are beyond our control. Why shoulder all the blame?"

He gave a rueful smile. "I was the sole survivor. But that's not the crux of it. The critical point is that I ordered a course change before the disaster struck. When the ship sank, it was 20 miles off the normal route. That decision was mine."

I was taken aback by his revelation, momentarily lost for words.

A captain altering course without just cause, leading to a shipwreck, cannot easily escape accountability.

Should Moore's decision be deemed a misjudgment, it would likely spell the end of his career at sea.

I studied him for a long while before asking, "What prompted you to change the usual route?"

Moore drew a deep breath. "I explained my reason to the investigation court, but they dismissed it. That's why I've come to you."

I couldn't help but smile wryly, thinking, How can I possibly influence the court's decision?

Moore met my gaze intently. His expression was so sincere that it could compel anyone to believe him. "Mr. Morris," he said, "I saw a ghost ship."

The words jolted me. "What?" I exclaimed.

He repeated himself, his voice steady and calm. "I saw a ghost ship."

I found myself gesturing wildly, wanting to refute his claim, yet no words came.

To clarify, the term "ghost ship" refers to a sunken vessel that inexplicably appears on the water's surface under certain conditions.

Though science offers no explanation for such phenomena, there are numerous accounts from witnesses — primarily sailors of the 18th and 19th centuries — who vividly described these apparitions. However, in the 20th century, credible records of "ghost ships" have all but vanished.

I halted my gesturing, and Moore asked, "Do you know what a ghost ship is?"

I nodded, still grappling for words.

Seeing my struggle, Moore continued, "I wasn't the only one who saw it. The first mate witnessed it too. But sadly, I'm the sole survivor, and no one believes me."

Finally, I found my voice. "What exactly happened at that moment?"

Moore recounted, "It was one in the morning. The first mate was on duty and spotted the ghost ship first. I was still awake, reading. He knocked on my door urgently, and when I opened it, he pulled me outside. Together, we saw three Spanish three-masted sailing ships directly in our path. If we continued on course, we would have collided with them!"

I shook my head, responding, "Surely you realize there are no such ships on the seas today."

Moore's smile was tinged with bitterness.

He paused before continuing, "The night was dark, and a thick fog hung over the sea. The ships were so close. I didn't stop to question it; I ordered a course change to the west to avoid them. But as we turned, the ships remained ahead, as if steering us further west. Within twenty minutes, we struck a reef."

I frowned, listening intently as Captain Moore spoke with conviction, yet my skepticism lingered.

Moore met my gaze, his expression resigned. "You probably think I'm unfit for command, don't you?"

I pondered how to approach this delicately, not wanting to deepen his despair, and remained silent for a moment. Finally, I ventured, "The 'ghost ship' phenomenon is often attributed to illusions. Even when multiple people perceive it simultaneously, it doesn't confirm a ship's presence. The vastness of the ocean can play tricks on the mind, leading to shared hallucinations."

From his expression, Moore listened with a patience born of desperation.

When I finished, disappointment clouded his features.

He took several deep gulps of his drink, clearly disheartened. "I had hoped for a different perspective from you. Forget it!" he sighed, setting his glass down with a decisive thud as he rose to his feet.

I looked up at him, my curiosity piqued. "What exactly are you implying?"

Moore leaned over the table, his hands planted firmly. "I assure you, it was no illusion. Three large masted sailing ships forced my vessel westward."

I remained silent, holding his gaze.

His voice rose with fervor, and his words cut through the air sharply. "Yet you, with your so-called expertise, tell me it was all in my head. Let me be clear, Mr. Morris, I've spent more time at sea than you've spent on land. I know the difference between illusion and reality!"

I sighed, sensing his unyielding conviction. It seemed I had little to offer that would sway him.

His frustration spilled over. "You're just like the so-called experts at the investigative court. They dismiss my account as mere hallucinations, dissecting it from every psychological and physical angle to conclude that I'm unfit for command."

His fist crashed down on the table, sending bottles and glasses rattling. The entire bar turned to witness the commotion.

I felt my own temper flare and stood abruptly. "If the investigative court reached that decision, perhaps it was justified."

Moore leaned in, eyes ablaze, as if challenging me. Though small in stature, his intensity was palpable. "Hmph, you think you're ready for my truth? It'll shock you!"

I scoffed, "Say what you will, I'm not easily frightened."

With determination in his voice, Moore declared, "I intend to prove those ships are real. I'm going back there!"

I retorted, "And how do you plan to prove the existence of ghost ships?"

"Ghosts have origins," Moore insisted. "Where there are ghosts, there are the dead. Where there are ghost ships, there must be sunken vessels. I've located those three sunken ships!"

I scrutinized him, and he snorted in frustration. "No point in explaining further to you. You're just like the rest!"

As Moore turned to leave, I instinctively reached out, grasping his arm. "What exactly were you hoping to accomplish by meeting with me?" I asked.

He chuckled, though there was a hint of bitterness in his laughter. "I was naive, I suppose. Initially, I thought... well, I wanted to ask you to join me on this venture."

His words caught me off guard. "Oh," I replied, taken aback, "I appreciate the confidence you have in me and the invitation."

Moore waved dismissively. "I was certain you'd agree. I even went through considerable effort to gather information about those three ships. But now... there's no point in discussing it."

I hesitated for a moment before gesturing for him to sit again. "Please, let's start over," I urged.

He paused, scrutinizing me, and I continued, "I can't promise anything right now because your story sounds outlandish, but I'm willing to hear what you've found."

After a long pause, Moore sat back down, his demeanor softening. "I apologize for my earlier behavior. I came here with hope, and when that hope seemed dashed —" He spread his hands, leaving the sentence unfinished.

I smiled gently. "No harm done, at least we haven't resorted to blows yet."

Moore's eyes narrowed with amusement, and I added, "Even if we did, it wouldn't matter. Convince me, and I'll admit I was wrong."

His laughter, though tinged with bitterness, carried a hint of relief.

"You mentioned you found information on the three ships? That seems impossible," I challenged.

Moore nodded, "I did see the three ships, and what struck me were the emblems on their bows."

He paused, gathering his thoughts. "I've been drawn to the sea since childhood, determined to make it my life's work. I've devoured countless books on sailing and tales of ancient explorers. The shield-shaped emblems on those ships seemed familiar. Afterward, I delved into research and found what I was looking for."

His passion was evident, and despite the strangeness of his claim, I felt compelled to hear more.

Chapter 2

The Quest for the "Ghost Ship"

As Moore spoke, he rummaged through his briefcase and retrieved a piece of yellowed paper, placing it on the table before us.

On both sides of the sea monster are patterns of spears, bows and arrows, oars and cannons. The whole picture seems to be printed with simple woodcut.

The paper, aged with time, bore a shield-shaped emblem at its center—a strange sea monster with wings, flanked by an array of spears, bows and arrows, oars, and cannons. The image seemed to be crafted with a simple woodcut technique, evoking a sense of antiquity.

Pointing to the emblem, Moore explained, "I discovered this in a historic library, renowned for its comprehensive collection of maritime records. This emblem belongs to the Degado family, an honor bestowed by Spanish Emperor Ferdinand V. The family has a storied legacy of service to the Spanish Navy."

Even with my limited knowledge of maritime history, the name Ferdinand V struck a chord. This was the same emperor who had championed Columbus's voyage, leading to the monumental discovery of the New World.

Sensing my skepticism, Moore spoke with renewed conviction. "I swear, the three ships I encountered bore these emblems on their bows. The copper crests stood about a meter tall. I couldn't mistake them, not for anything."

As I examined the paper, my mind entertained the possibility that Moore's memory was playing tricks on him — perhaps he'd encountered the emblem in his studies, and it lingered in his subconscious only to manifest as an illusion. Similar phenomena occur in dreams, where the mind conjures forgotten images and experiences.

However, voicing such doubts would likely stir unnecessary conflict, so I merely nodded. "This does seem like credible information."

Moore's enthusiasm was palpable. "This is just the beginning. Take a look at this record!"

He produced another book, equally ancient, its pages inscribed in Spanish.

Turning to a specific page, he pointed to an insert. "Look at this illustration."

The insert depicted three massive three-masted ships, their bows adorned with the very emblems we had just discussed.

"The book recounts that in 1503, a year after Columbus charted Central America, three of the Degado family's finest captains each helmed a three-masted ship. With 150 sailors and soldiers aboard, they reached Puerto Rico, left their forces behind, and continued their voyage northward."

Moore paused, his eyes searching mine for a reaction.

As Moore spoke, I quickly skimmed through the records in the book. It detailed how the Degado family embarked on their voyage with hopes of discovering another Central America or perhaps an entirely new world. Yet, they vanished, the three ships never returning after departing from Puerto Rico.

Moore waited patiently as I absorbed the information. Once I finished, he leaned forward, a sense of urgency in his voice. "Do you see now? These three ships sank in the Atlantic!"

I closed the book, nodding. "Since they disappeared after setting out, it's logical to assume they met their fate in the Atlantic."

Moore continued, "Back then, there was no communication equipment, no radar. Sailing was fraught with danger. All anyone knew was that these ships vanished. As for where, when, and how they sank, it's a mystery."

I acknowledged his point. "Yes, maritime history is filled with such tragedies."

"But I know where these three ships sank!" Moore declared, his determination palpable.

I frowned, intrigued yet skeptical.

He struck the table with conviction. "Where I saw them is where they went down!"

I studied him. "So, you're convinced that the wrecks are still there on the seafloor, and you intend to find them?"

Moore nodded emphatically, "Yes, I'm certain those are the ships I saw."

I pondered the situation. Perhaps Moore did see something resembling the Degado family ships, but the same psychological explanations could suggest it was a hallucination.

Moore waited, searching my face for a response. "Do you think my evidence is convincing enough?"

Leaning back, I asked, "If we locate a sunken ship, will it benefit your sailing career?"

He sighed, a mix of hope and resignation in his voice. "The investigation court might still dismiss the 'ghost ship' explanation, but at least I'll know I'm not an unreliable captain prone to hallucinations."

I understood how crucial this was for Moore's peace of mind and future. "If you're intent on finding the wrecks, you'll need a ship and the right equipment."

Moore's eyes lit up, his excitement uncontainable. "I have them! I told you my promotion was based on merit, but my father is also the chairman of a major shipping company."

I nodded. "So, he's helping you?"

"Yes," Moore affirmed. "We talked through the night, and he agreed to support me. He's provided a high-performance yacht suitable for ocean voyages, along with ample diving and detection gear."

I hesitated, wanting to be transparent. "I should mention, I'm not an experienced diver."

Moore grasped my hand with a firm grip. "That's not the issue. What's important is that you're willing to entertain this possibility, and that's enough!"

I felt a twinge of guilt, as my skepticism lingered. Yet, seeing Moore's earnestness, I couldn't bring myself to voice my doubts.

"So, who else have you enlisted to help us?" I inquired.

"There's just one more person," Moore replied. "He'll meet us in Puerto Rico. You might have heard of him—Mr. Mellon, the most renowned diver in the Atlantic."

I perked up at the name. "Not only have I heard of him, but I've also met him. Though I thought he'd retired!"

Moore nodded. "He did retire last year, but I've persuaded him to lend his expertise."

I frowned slightly. Diving is notoriously perilous, and at 38, Mr. Mellon is considered old for the profession. After half a year of retirement, could he still endure the physical demands? However, I kept my concerns to myself, trusting that Mellon knew his limits.

Moore's excitement was palpable. "Imagine it — Mellon, you, and I. Together, we'll find those ships. I know what I saw; they exist!"

I hesitated. "I'm not well-versed in sailing, and ghost ships are a mystery to me. Are you suggesting ghost ships are real?"

Moore shook his head. "Not at all."

"Then forgive my curiosity," I pressed. "When you encountered those ancient ships, why didn't you simply sail through, assuming they were illusions?"

Pain flickered across Moore's face. "When we hit the reef, I realized I could have done just that. But in the moment, I acted on instinct to avoid them. I had no time to think."

I took a deep breath. "So you're suggesting that when a ghost ship appears, some mysterious force clouds judgment, compelling one to act irrationally?"

Moore frowned, lowering his gaze. After a moment, he looked up again. "I can't explain it."

He paused before asking, "Are you afraid?"

I laughed, clapping him on the shoulder. "I've committed to this, fear or not. Where's your ship docked? I'll meet you there the morning after tomorrow."

Moore beamed. "Great! The ship is docked near Pier 3, named 'Maurice.' You'll spot it easily at the dock. I'll be waiting!"

With that, our first meeting concluded. We parted ways at the bar's entrance.

Over the next day and a half, I busied myself preparing my gear and immersing myself in research, eager to uncover whatever truths the sea held.

In preparation for our voyage, I delved into the history of Spanish navigation. I discovered that the book Moore had shown me must be a rare, out-of-print edition, as mentions of the Degado family were scarce in other texts. The only reference I found labeled them as traitors, likely a result of political machinations that led to their erasure from history.

I also researched Mr. Mellon, our diving expert. The information confirmed that he was indeed one of the best divers globally, renowned for his skill and experience.

On the morning of our meeting, I arrived at the dock at 8 a.m. Before I even located the "Maurice," Moore came sprinting toward me, his face glistening with sweat. Grabbing my hand with earnest relief, he exclaimed, "You came! You can't imagine how worried I was, afraid you'd change your mind!"

I couldn't help but smile at his sincerity. "It seems you have more faith in ghost ships than in people. You expect the ghost ship to be waiting for you, yet you feared I'd not show up."

Moore chuckled awkwardly. "I didn't mean it that way. I just worried that once you thought it over, you'd decide it was all too far-fetched and back out."

As we walked toward the dock, I reassured him, "To be honest, I've always thought it improbable. But even if it's just an adventure, I'm in. It's not every day I get a travel companion like you."

Moore's spirits lifted. "I requested an extension from the investigation court, arguing that I'm gathering evidence to prove the accident wasn't my fault. They've granted me one and a half months."

"That sounds sufficient," I agreed.

Moore took my luggage as we approached the "Maurice." At first glance, an inexplicable dislike for the ship washed over me—though time would prove it to be an exceptional vessel. Its appearance was unconventional, seemingly crafted to mimic a Maori canoe. Yet, Moore's enthusiasm for the "Maurice" was palpable. As we boarded, he eagerly asked, "What do you think of the ship?"

"It looks quite unusual, doesn't it?" I replied.

Moore led me to the cabin, his hands affectionately caressing the ship's gleaming copper fittings as if tending to a cherished child. When we stepped inside, I was taken aback. The cabin was nothing like I had expected.

The "Maurice" was modest in size, featuring a single cabin layout that felt surprisingly spacious. At the back, two double beds were positioned against the bulkhead. In the center, a long table was flanked by four chairs on either side, while the helm was situated near the bow.

Diving equipment was neatly stacked within the cabin, giving it an air of readiness for our expedition. Moore placed my belongings on one of the beds and turned to me with a grin. "We'll be setting off shortly. You'll pick up the basics of sailing quickly. With such a long journey ahead, the three of us will need to share the helm. There are plenty of books onboard to keep us entertained during our time at sea," he noted, gesturing to several large wooden crates.

I silently made my way to the helm, inspecting the controls. As Moore explained the ship's operations, he fired up the engine, and we began our journey. The "Maurice" eased away from the dock and soon we were out at sea.

The endless expanse of the sea seemed to meld time, each day flowing seamlessly into the next, driven by the undulating waves and the steady drone of the engine. One twilight, as the sun dipped below the horizon, casting an amber glow, Moore and I delved into the mystery surrounding the Degado family.

"Is your book on the Degado family the only known copy?" I queried, my curiosity piqued. "I've combed through countless tomes on Spanish maritime history and found not a single mention of them. It's as though they've been deliberately erased from history."

Moore nodded. "Yes, it's shrouded in mystery. It's as if all traces of the family were deliberately erased."

Curious, I asked, "Where did your book come from?"

Moore shrugged. "It's always been on my father's bookshelf. I've known their emblem since childhood. As for the book's origins, only my father might know."

I didn't press further. The Degado family's past, while intriguing, wasn't our primary focus.

During our voyage, I immersed myself in the books Moore had brought aboard, each page a new chapter in the rich tapestry of maritime history. These tales of the sea, filled with daring exploits and ancient navigational wisdom, transformed my understanding. By the time we reached Puerto Rico ten days later, I felt more like a seasoned sailor than a novice.

Mr. Mellon, our diving expert who joined us there, took note of my newfound competence. "You've got the air of someone who's spent a lifetime at sea," he remarked, nodding appreciatively. It was a testament to the knowledge I'd absorbed from those volumes, and it made me feel more prepared for the challenges that lay ahead on our journey into the mysterious waters of the Atlantic.

As we set sail northward into the vast Atlantic, the mood shifted to one of anticipation. Mellon, with his robust frame and fiery red hair, claimed Viking ancestry, a fact he was more than happy to share. His boisterous personality made him easy to get along with, and the three of us formed a tight-knit group.

Mellon and I focused on our work, ensuring the diving equipment was in perfect condition, but Moore's nerves were on edge as we approached the location of the "ghost ship" sighting.

On the fourth morning, Moore was on night watch while Mellon and I slept. We were abruptly awakened by Moore's urgent voice, "Get up quickly."

Groggy and disoriented, we caught sight of the anxious glint in his eyes. Dawn's feeble light scarcely pierced the dense gray fog that shrouded the sea. Moore had cut the engine, leaving the "Maurice" to drift silently, eerily. The stillness was haunting, fractured only by the oppressive fog swirling around us.

Mellon and I exchanged puzzled glances. "What's going on?" I asked.

"Don't make any sound. Just listen!" Moore whispered, his tension palpable.

We strained our ears but heard nothing distinctive. I was about to speak when Moore motioned for silence, urging us to listen further.

I shrugged at Mellon; the sea seemed tranquil, with no unusual sounds.

After a pause, Moore insisted, "Can't you hear it? The sound of seawater hitting the bow."

Listening intently, I picked up on a faint "pat" sound— waves lapping against a hull. It was a normal sound, I thought, assuming it was the "Maurice."

"We're on the ship, Moore. The sea is hitting the 'Maurice,'" I said quietly.

Moore shook his head. "No, this is different. There's a distinct sound when a ship's moving versus when it's stationary. I can tell."

Mellon, visibly tense, whispered, "So, there's a ship nearby?"

Moore nodded, "Yes, and judging by the sound, it's moving at about three nautical miles."

He paused, adding, "That's the typical speed of a fifteenth-century three-masted sailing ship!"

A shiver ran down my spine as I absorbed his words. Mellon, more on edge, murmured, "A ghost ship?"

Moore stood motionless, his silence more chilling than the fog that enveloped us. I strained my eyes, but the dense mist cloaked his figure in an impenetrable shroud. Moore's words lingered, igniting a spark of awareness within me. The faint, rhythmic "pat pat" I had dismissed as the sound of our bow slicing through the water was now unmistakably coming from the depths of the mist. The source was out there, hidden, yet undeniably real. The air grew thick with an unspoken tension, and my senses heightened, attuned to every murmur of the unseen.

"How did you notice such a faint sound?" I asked, intrigued by Moore's perceptiveness.

Moore stayed focused on the fog. "Intuition," he replied. "I just felt another ship was near."

I stood resolute. "Alright, let's stop guessing. Get the fog lights. I'll go to the bow and signal. If there's another ship nearby, it should see us."

Mellon's voice trembled as he whispered, "But if it's a ghost ship—"

Before he could finish, I cut in sharply, "Let's get one thing straight, Moore. Ghost ships? They belong in tales and legends. I refuse to believe in their existence!"

With determination, I turned away, seizing the fog light and stepping onto the deck. The fog was so thick I could scarcely make out the bow of the "Maurice." Moving cautiously, I edged forward, stopping against the bulkhead. Hoisting the fog light high, I began sending signals, the simplest message—Please answer me!

The orange-yellow beam sliced through the dense fog as I repeated the message several times, pausing to scan the mist for any response. The fog remained unyielding, a relentless wall of white with no sign of a return signal.

As I prepared to send another signal, a voice startled me from behind. "It's no use, they're gone!" It was Moore's voice, though his figure was still lost in the fog. The realization that the sound of seawater hitting the hull had changed confirmed his words.

The thick mist seemed to close in tighter, suffocating any remaining hope.

Turning, I nearly collided with Moore, who stood close behind. His face was pale, ghostly in the eerie light. From the cabin, Mellon's voice rang out, "Come and see!"

We rushed back inside, relieved by the cabin's comparative clarity. Mellon clutched a long strip of paper—the radar scan. He pointed to a spike among the steady lines and declared, "Look, the radar recorded a ship approaching us."

I shook my head, skeptical. "If the radar can detect ghosts, that would be a miracle!"

Moore's voice sliced through the tension, sharp with disbelief. "Then, what was it?"

"Probably a big fish," I suggested, though the cabin's sudden silence spoke volumes. Both Moore and Mellon seemed more inclined to believe in ghost ships than my rational explanation. I chose to let the matter rest.

As the silence lingered, the fog outside began to dissipate gradually, revealing more of the sea around us. I broke the quiet, asking, "Moore, we're almost at our destination, right?"

After a pause, Moore replied, "Not almost there— we're already here."

I moved to the control panel and pressed the button. The sound of iron chains loosening echoed from the side of the boat as the anchor deployed. The ship rocked gently, then settled into a calm stillness. Taking a deep breath, I declared, "We've reached our destination. It's time to dive!"

Moore and Mellon exchanged glances, a silent communication passing between them. I broke the silence, my voice steady, "It's time to deploy the submarine detector as well."

The "Maurice" was equipped with cutting-edge submarine detection technology, an invaluable tool for uncovering shipwrecks hidden beneath the waves. If the detector picked up metal on the seabed, it likely marked the resting place of a long-lost vessel.

Moore exhaled deeply, a hint of apprehension in his voice, "Alright, let's begin. May Providence be on our side."

With deft fingers, he manipulated the control panel, bringing a dark green fluorescent screen to life. Lines of light danced across it, stretching from one end to the other in a mesmerizing pattern.

Mellon paced restlessly, his impatience palpable. "We need to dive," he declared. "Seeing it with our own eyes is the only way we'll uncover anything."

His confidence was infectious, rooted in years of salvaging ancient wrecks. "Ships that have lain beneath the waves for centuries are often buried in sand," he explained. "Even if fragments of metal pierce the surface, they've likely corroded to the point that the detector only whispers of their presence."

I nodded, acknowledging the truth in his words.

The thick fog gathered and dispersed quickly over the sea. In that moment, I glanced outside, greeted by a vast expanse of blue water and clear sky.

Peering through the cabin window, I saw the sea stretching endless and empty to the horizon. Moore noticed my gaze and murmured, "It's long gone," as if reading my thoughts.

I pondered aloud, "If a ship were moving at three knots, shouldn't we still see it?"

Moore met my eyes, his expression inscrutable. "Ghost ships do not reveal themselves under the sun."

I considered pressing the point but reasoned it was a futile argument. Instead, I chuckled, "Next time I hear such sounds, I'll launch a boat and follow them to their source."

Moore's face paled, his demeanor shifting to one of grave sincerity. "If you chase a ghost ship, you might vanish without a trace," he warned. He paused, his words hanging heavy in the air. "Then, in time, the ghost ship will reappear. Perhaps you'd find yourself toiling on its decks."

The absurdity of it almost drew a laugh from me, yet I restrained myself, aware that such levity might invite misfortune. I jested lightly, "Well, perhaps that means an eternal existence, beyond life's usual bounds?"

Moore frowned, his mind grappling with the concept. A silence settled until Mellon's voice cut through, commanding and urgent, "Enough talk! We must act. One diver at a time, no more than 500 yards, then we move the boat."

We nodded in agreement, our resolve crystallizing into action. Together, we lowered an underwater propeller into the sea—a deceptively simple device, yet indispensable for submarine exploration. Fitted with propellers fore and aft, it was bolstered by spare oxygen tanks and a formidable speargun. A powerful battery drove it, a lamp piercing the ocean's depths with its beam. Though not swift by sea's standards, the propeller outpaced human swimmers, conserving precious energy.

Mellon, already donning his oxygen tank, proclaimed with a grin, "I'll take the first dive."

When Mellon declared his intent to dive, neither Moore nor I saw any cause for concern. Mellon was a seasoned diver, and with our radio walkie-talkies, we could maintain constant communication. We kept a prudent distance of 500 meters, ensuring maximum safety.

Mellon limbered up on the deck, his movements fluid and practiced, before he plunged into the sea.

The fog had lifted that day, revealing a sun-drenched sky. The sun's rays were relentless, scorching our skin, and casting brilliant glints on the water's surface. The sea was astonishingly clear, allowing us to track Mellon's descent. About three meters down, he aligned himself with the propeller. It churned the water into twin spirals as Mellon glided forward, gradually descending.

Though trusting his honed instincts, Mellon didn't let his guard down. He promptly established contact with us Wearing the waterproof hood enabled him to converse with us underwater.

His voice crackled over the radio, "I'm at 30 meters. The sea's placid. At 50 meters, visibility remains high. At 70 meters, it seems this area's not too deep."

Moore glanced at the data streaming from the recorder. "We're about 200 meters above the seabed," he reported.

Mellon's voice rose again, infused with curiosity, "I'm descending further. If a ship went down here, a sudden storm must've been the cause. I see reefs below, draped in seaweed."

I cautioned, "Mellon, watch out. Records show shark sightings in this area."

Mellon chuckled, "No sharks yet, but there's a succulent lobster and a stonefish. I'll grab a few for lunch when I surface. It's incredible down here. Makes me question my retirement thoughts. Last time was just a fluke."

We understood the weight of his words. His retirement decision stemmed from a harrowing incident—trapped in a submerged cave for 48 hours. A pocket of air had been his only salvation, but even then, his rescue landed him in the hospital for over a month.

Mellon's mention of that ordeal cast a shadow over our mood, Moore and I exchanging uneasy glances.

Yet, we stayed silent. The weather was perfect, and with Mellon's expertise, a 200-meter dive was as routine as crossing an empty street—devoid of danger.

His voice returned, tinged with awe, "I've reached the seabed. The sand is fine and white. It's endless, like an underwater desert, Moore!"

Chapter 3

Hidden Mysteries

Mellon's sudden call echoed through the radio, snapping Moore to attention. "What's the matter?" he responded, his voice taut with concern.

"From what I can tell," Mellon relayed, "in situations like this, either the shipwreck's entirely buried beneath the sand, making it nearly impossible to locate, or it stands fully exposed, waiting to be discovered."

"Let's hope it's the latter," Moore murmured, his eyes fixed on the horizon.

"If there's a shipwreck at all," I interjected, unable to resist a touch of skepticism.

Moore shot me a playful glare, to which I responded with a knowing grin. I reclined on a canvas chair, unfurled the parasol, and let the soothing sea breeze wash over me. Moore was handling communications with Mellon, so I allowed myself to drift into sleep, lulled by the gentle rocking of the ship.

As I began to fade into slumber, their voices wove a comforting background hum, but soon, even that faded into dreams.

The rhythmic sway of the boat and the caress of the breeze had drawn me into a deep sleep. When I awoke, I was jolted upright. The sun, once low in the sky, now hung at its zenith, casting intense rays upon the ocean.

I sprang from the chair, scanning the deck for Moore. He was nowhere to be seen. A glance at my watch revealed the time: past midday. I had been asleep for over three hours.

A sense of unease prickled at the edges of my awareness. "Moore, should Mellon surface by now?" I called, the unease creeping into my voice.

Silence.

I stood, my gaze falling to the small radio intercom perched precariously on the ship's edge. Picking it up, I was greeted by a faint, yet distinct, "rustling" — the unmistakable whisper of water.

Dread coiled in my stomach. The sound signaled that the other half of the intercom was submerged, still with Mellon. He should not have been underwater for this long. We had planned to rotate shifts.

Urgency surged through me. "Moore!" I called again, my voice edged with panic.

No response. The air felt heavy, oppressive.

I pressed the button on the intercom, my voice steady but urgent, "Mellon, what's happening?"

In place of an answer, rhythmic knocking echoed through the intercom, each tap resonating with eerie persistence.

Despite the sun's blazing intensity, a chill gripped my entire being as I yelled, "Moore, what are you doing?" My voice echoed into the empty sea as I dashed toward the ship's cabin. In the confined space of the "Maurice," it was immediately clear—Moore was nowhere inside.

He wasn't in the cabin, nor on the deck. The realization struck me with brutal simplicity: Moore was not on the ship.

I stood frozen, rooted by shock. My mind reeled, my scalp tingling with dread, my legs threatening to buckle beneath me. The radio walkie-talkie, slick with sweat in my grip, continued its eerie "pat"—a sound unmistakably like nails being driven into wood.

For half a minute, I remained paralyzed, until a primal scream tore from my throat. Whether I called for Moore or Mellon, I can't recall—I simply screamed. Sometimes, an instinctive cry is the only tether to sanity, a way to reclaim thought from chaos. And in that moment, clarity began to seep back in.

Breath ragged, I struggled to piece together the sequence of events. Mellon had dived first, and I had drifted into sleep, lulled by the tranquility of the day. But tranquility had been shattered; when I awoke, Moore was gone.

It was irrefutable—Moore was no longer aboard. The boat lay stagnant in the vast sea. If not on the vessel, he must be in the water. Yet, no sign of him on the surface, which meant only one thing: he was beneath the waves.

This stark realization required a scream to surface, but it finally crystallized in my mind. Moore must have dived into the sea.

With urgency, I inspected the storage area for our diving equipment. My worst fears were confirmed. A critical set of diving gear was missing: an oxygen tank, a hood, and a submarine propeller.

Moore had descended into the depths, and it was a decision made in haste—his remaining gear was a jumbled chaos, evidence of his hurried departure. What could have driven him to such a rash decision? The question hung heavy in the air, as I pieced together the puzzle of his sudden plunge into the unknown.

As I lay in the depths of a deep slumber, the world around me faded into silence. The noise he made did not rouse me from my sleep, which was not unusual. What puzzled me was why Moore had chosen not to wake me.

In that calm moment, clarity washed over me. The fact that Moore hadn't disturbed my rest was oddly reassuring. It suggested that, despite the haste of his actions, there was no imminent danger. Surely, if peril loomed, Moore would have had every reason to wake me.

With only two courses of action before me—waiting for their return on the boat or diving into the depths to find them—I chose the latter. I reached for a cylinder of oxygen, donned my diving hood, and stepped out of the cabin.

No sooner had I emerged than a splash disturbed the calm sea near the boat. A figure rose from the water.

The hood obscured my vision, leaving me uncertain if it was Moore or Mellon. Yet, the sight of someone emerging from the water sent a thrill of anticipation through me. I shouted across the water, "Hey, what happened?"

The figure pulled off his hood—it was Mellon. His face, ghostly pale, struck me with concern. But then, he'd likely been in the sea for over three hours, and even the strongest of men would appear pale under such circumstances.

I watched Mellon swim toward the boat and called out again, "Where's Moore?"

Mellon remained silent, reaching the boat's ladder and pulling himself aboard with a deep breath.

Before I could press further, another splash broke the surface, and another figure appeared. It could only be Moore.

Relief flooded over me as both of them surfaced. Moments ago, panic had gripped me like a vice, the world teetering on the brink of chaos. Now, it all seemed almost comical.

I rushed to the ladder, extending a hand to help Mellon first, then Moore. Once aboard, Moore removed his hood, revealing a pallor that matched Mellon's.

I turned to Moore, my voice tinged with accusation, "Hey, why did you go down without a word while I slept?"

Moore met my gaze with a wry smile, remaining silent. His expression was enigmatic. I glanced at Mellon, finding the same inscrutable look.

The two exchanged a glance, a silent pact hanging between them. A secret, clearly meant to exclude me, the only other person there.

A wave of irritation swelled within me, mingling with my curiosity. Naturally, I felt slighted. Moore had sought me out, implying a willingness to work together openly. Yet here he was, sharing knowing glances with Mellon, keeping secrets.

My displeasure must have been written all over my face, for Moore quickly addressed it. "You were sleeping deeply," he explained, "so I didn't wake you."

I didn't let it go. "Didn't we agree to take turns going into the water? Why did Mellon go in, and why did you follow?"

My gaze bore into Moore, my tone sharp, demanding answers. He averted his eyes, his voice trailing off, "I just wanted to check the situation in the sea—"

Abruptly, he shifted the conversation. "By the way, we should report our location to the nearest port, just in case—"

He barely took a step before I caught his shoulder. "Hold on. I have questions."

His frown deepened as he turned to face me. "You seemed in a hurry when you went into the water. What happened?"

He blinked, momentarily caught off guard. "What happened? Nothing happened."

He called out to Mellon, "Nothing happened, right?"

Mellon, who had been slouched on the canvas chair, straightened abruptly as if jolted. "Yes, nothing, of course nothing!"

But their performance was unconvincing, fueling my irritation. Their rehearsed responses were clumsy, treating me like a fool.

I masked my anger with a sardonic smile. "When I woke, the radio intercom was on the deck, and there was a noise like hammering nails coming through it. What was that?"

Mellon hesitated, thinking before he spoke. "Oh, perhaps it was the intercom hitting the propeller."

If Mellon hadn't brought up the propeller, the detail might have slipped my mind. But his mention jolted me. "I just checked," I said, my voice tinged with urgency, "and we're missing two submarine propellers. Where did they go?"

The question hung in the air, heavy with implication. Moore and Mellon exchanged a brief silence before Moore responded, "Ash, what are you doubting?"

His question was an invitation, freeing me to voice my growing unease. I raised my voice, no longer containing my frustration. "I'm not doubting — I'm certain! You encountered something in the sea and are hiding it from me!"

I expected my blunt accusation to unsettle Moore, but he remained unruffled, a composure that was unexpected and unsettling. He turned his gaze to the serene expanse of the sea, his voice calm and measured. "You're too suspicious."

Despite my intuition suggesting that Moore's calmness in the face of my direct accusation might indicate a clear conscience, his response left me feeling awkward about pressing further. As Moore retreated into the cabin, I glanced at Mellon, who reclined once more on the canvas chair, eyes ostensibly closed. Yet his twitching eyelids betrayed the turmoil within, indicating that something weighed heavily on his mind.

My mood darkened swiftly. Moore and Mellon were clearly hiding something, and the realization left me simmering with anger. It's a natural reaction when one discovers deceit from supposed allies. Yet, strangely, amid the anger, I found it almost humorous. This entire venture had little to do with me. I had embarked on this journey at Moore's insistence, never truly believing in the "ghost ship" legend. Even if we uncovered the sunken ship, what would I gain? I was merely assisting, yet they chose to deceive me. Why should I continue?

A laugh escaped me, sharp and mirthless. Mellon's eyes snapped open, surprise etched on his face. Ignoring him, I moved toward the cabin.

Inside, Moore sat at the communication station. I flopped onto the bed with a sigh. "When you contact the nearest port, you might as well ask for a seaplane," I suggested, my tone casual. "I'm done chasing sunken ships."

Moore turned, blinking at me. "The port warned of an approaching storm," he said, his voice steady. "We should head back at full speed."

His words caught me off guard. While sudden weather shifts are not unheard of, we should have had some forewarning. It seemed more an excuse than a genuine concern. Why the rush back after just one dive?

Ordinarily, I'd demand answers, but I had resolved to distance myself from their venture. Whatever their secrets, they no longer concerned me. "Fine," I replied lazily. "Let's go while the weather holds." Moore nodded, pressing a button to retrieve the anchor, the mechanical clatter filling the air.

In that moment, Moore unwittingly exposed a flaw in their story. Claiming to learn of the storm after contacting the port, he should have informed Mellon. Yet, without a word to Mellon, he prepared to set sail. Clearly, their plans were prearranged.

I suppressed a bitter smile, choosing silence over confrontation. Their actions spoke volumes about their character.

For the next two days, words were scarce between us, the atmosphere aboard the ship growing increasingly tense and unpleasant. I avoided them as much as possible, unable to bear their silent communication and secretive glances.

The moment we docked at Puerto Rico, I seized the opportunity to leave. With no intention of lingering, I boarded a small commercial plane bound for the United States, eager to put distance between myself and their deceit.

Moore and Mellon escorted me to the plane, but I carried my own luggage, offering them not so much as a farewell. As the plane ascended, a wave of relief washed over me. I was finally free from those duplicitous and hypocritical individuals.

Yet, as relief settled in, regret followed. The days spent on this fruitless expedition felt like the most wasted period of my life. I briefly wondered if Moore and Mellon would carry on their mysterious venture after seeing me off, but quickly dismissed the thought. It was no longer my concern, and I resolved to forget I had ever crossed paths with Moore.

Reflecting on my initial impression of Moore, I couldn't help but chuckle at how misleading first impressions can be. Upon returning home, I checked the weather reports. There was no mention of any storm over the Atlantic. Moore had fabricated the whole story, further tarnishing my view of him.

And just like that, the chapter was closed.

Twenty days passed, and the incident receded from my mind until a headline caught my eye. In a sports magazine, a report detailed the shocking suicide of Mellon, a renowned diving expert. The revelation stunned me. For a moment, I hoped it was a case of mistaken identity.

But the journalist's work was thorough. The article included numerous photos of Mellon, confirming his identity beyond doubt. Among them, a haunting image showed Mellon lying lifeless on the floor, a rifle clutched in his hand.

The report detailed how Mellon had tied a rope to the rifle's bolt, aimed the muzzle at his chin, and pulled the rope, ensuring a fatal shot to the brain. The method spoke volumes about his resolve to end his life.

The news left me shaken, stirring a mix of disbelief and sorrow. Though I had distanced myself from Mellon and his secrets, the tragedy of his end lingered with me, a stark reminder of the darkness that sometimes lurks beneath the surface.

The date of Mellon's suicide caught my eye, and I was stunned. He had taken his life just six days after we parted ways in Puerto Rico. If he had returned home on the "Maurice," it meant he ended his life almost immediately upon reaching home.

I reread the detailed report. It confirmed that Mellon had indeed committed suicide shortly after a long journey. His neighbors reported that he'd been away for about half a month, but none knew his destination. Interestingly, they remarked on his good spirits before he left, recalling his cheerful conversations.

The journalist discovered that Mellon had purchased a plane ticket to Puerto Rico, but from there, his trail went cold. The article concluded with a haunting question: "What drove Mellon to suicide? Did his mysterious trip expose him to something unimaginable? It seems the mystery of Mellon's death may never be solved."

The report left me in a daze, for I knew what the journalist did not. Upon reaching Puerto Rico, Mellon had met me, and we embarked on the "Maurice" together. Our voyage, devoid of any real intrigue, took us near Bermuda, where we lingered for a mere four or five hours before departing.

From what I gathered, after I left, Moore and Mellon did not return to the site. Instead, they took Mellon directly back to the United States. If any "mystery" had prompted Mellon's suicide, it certainly wasn't the voyage itself.

Yet, I couldn't dismiss the memory of their odd expressions when they surfaced from the dive. What had they seen beneath the waves? Could something down there have driven Mellon to his tragic end?

My thoughts circled this puzzle endlessly until I resolved to contact Moore. Despite my disdain for his deceit, he might hold answers to Mellon's death.

Over twenty days had passed since the incident before I stumbled upon the magazine. Perhaps the local press hadn't deemed Mellon's death newsworthy enough, or perhaps it was buried in an inconspicuous section. If Moore had returned to New Zealand, he might still be unaware of Mellon's fate. Regardless, I needed to inform him, despicable as he was.

Recalling the shipping company Moore mentioned—where his father was chairman—I set out to find him. I contacted the telephone company, and within half an hour, they arranged a call to New Zealand. Twenty minutes later, the phone rang, and a voice with a thick Irish accent answered, "I'm Moore, Peter Moore."

Assuming he was Moore's father, I quickly explained, "I'm looking for Captain George Moore, who just returned from America."

There was a pause on the line before the voice asked, "Who are you?"

Chapter 4

One Was Dead, the Other Crazy

The moment was surreal as I introduced myself to Peter Moore over the phone, explaining how I had encountered his son. His voice shifted to urgency, surprising me. "Please wait for me. I will come to see you right away."

Confused, I replied, "Sir, you're in New Zealand, and I am—"

But he cut me off, "I will come to see you. I can get on the plane immediately!"

Alarmed, I asked, "What happened to Moore? Is there something wrong?"

His voice trembled with urgency. "Yes, I am his father."

"I figured as much. What's going on?" I pressed.

"He is crazy. I must come to see you. We'll discuss this in person, okay?"

The words "he is crazy" left me in shock. I could only stammer, "Okay," before the line went dead. I stood there, still clutching the phone, my mind racing.

Two thoughts dominated my mind. First, it seemed clear that even without my call, Peter Moore intended to contact me. His immediate decision to travel implied urgency. Second, I pondered the implication of "he's crazy." It could signify a mental breakdown, or it might mean George Moore had embarked on some irrational, fantastical venture. I hoped it was the latter—a whimsical notion rather than a complete mental collapse. With Mellon already gone, the thought of Moore losing his sanity was chilling.

I sat there, gradually regaining composure. With nothing to do but wait for Peter Moore's arrival, I revisited the magazine, reading the report on Mellon's suicide repeatedly. Mellon's life had been one of luxury, indicative of his success as a diver. The report painted a picture of a man who, despite living alone, was surrounded by opulence and numerous girlfriends, yet had never married or left a will.

The article's investigation concluded that Mellon had no apparent reason for suicide. He epitomized happiness, enjoying life to its fullest. If someone like Mellon found reason to end his life, what hope was there for anyone else?

Mellon wasn't a tortured thinker prone to existential despair. Instead, he embraced hedonism wholeheartedly. His suicide seemed unfathomable given his lifestyle.

As I spent the day gathering more information about Mellon's death, Peter Moore arrived the following noon.

Peter Moore stood before me, a stark contrast to his son—tall, thin, and exuding a restrained sadness that he struggled to mask. He carried himself with the gravitas of a successful man, perhaps a banker, and when he shook my hand, his bright eyes seemed to bore into mine, searching for answers.

I invited him to sit, and he wasted no time. "We don't need to waste time. George came back three days ago, and he's not himself. He's confused, a completely different person. I need to know what happened!"

His directness caught me off guard, and I hesitated. Seeing my reluctance, he pressed on, "If you don't tell me, I'll have to go to the United States to find Mr. Mellon. I know the three of you were together!"

Mentioning Mellon shocked me into action. "Mr. Mellon is dead. He committed suicide," I said, watching the disbelief widen his eyes. Though he refrained from speaking immediately, his expression suggested he doubted my words.

But Mellon's suicide was an undeniable fact, and I didn't feel the need to justify it further. Instead, I retrieved the magazine from the table and handed it to him, open to the article on Mellon's death.

He scanned the report silently, his breathing growing more labored. I waited patiently as he absorbed the grim details.

After ten minutes, he looked up, his voice trembling. "It's terrible!"

I nodded. "People commit suicide every day. It's not the act itself that's shocking, but the circumstances around it that are strange."

He planted his hands on his knees, trying to steady his shaking. "You didn't explain much on the phone. What happened to your son?"

His face twisted with grief. "He's crazy," he said, his voice barely above a whisper.

I remained silent, allowing him to continue. "His nerves are completely shattered. The doctors at the mental hospital said they've never seen a case as severe."

My heart pounded in my chest. "Mr. Moore, I didn't know your son well, but he struck me as confident and strong."

He gave a bitter smile. "I agree with you."

"People like that usually withstand shock and stress without breaking," I reasoned.

But Mr. Moore shook his head, his hands trembling as he rubbed his face. "The neurologists say everyone has a limit. If that limit is exceeded, even the strongest can crumble."

I grimaced. "So, what kind of shock did he encounter? Is it related to his inability to sail or an unfavorable court ruling?"

Again, he shook his head. "He's been granted a postponement for the trial. The court's decision is due today."

"So, what caused it?" I mused aloud.

He fixed me with a steady gaze. "That's why I'm here. I need to know what happened. Why is he like this?"

I could only offer a bitter smile and a shrug. "I don't know. I truly don't. I can't explain why Mellon took his own life or why your son is in this state. I can tell you what happened during our time together, but I doubt it will provide the clarity you seek."

"Then please, tell me," he urged.

With his earnest plea hanging in the air, I prepared to recount the events of our shared journey, knowing full well that the answers we both sought might remain elusive.

I paused to collect my thoughts, then poured a glass of wine for both of us before delving into the story.

Starting with the day Captain Moore and I first met, I recounted the events leading up to the dive. I kept the prelude brief, focusing instead on the pivotal moment when Mellon went into the water. I fell asleep, only to awaken and find both of them missing from the boat. Eventually, they surfaced, but something had clearly changed.

I relayed this part with emphasis, believing it to be the crux of the entire mystery. Whatever they encountered beneath the waves must have been so harrowing that it drove one to suicide and the other to madness.

As I finished, Peter Moore sat in silence, sipping his wine, absorbed in thought. After what felt like an eternity, I broke the silence. "I'm eager to understand his condition—what happened when he returned?"

Peter Moore's eyes darkened with sorrow. "He didn't truly come back," he said solemnly.

Confused, I pressed, "What do you mean?"

He explained, "The Maurice was discovered over 100 miles east of Sydney. It was adrift, unguided. When the crew boarded, they found him laughing maniacally."

A chill ran down my spine as Peter continued, "The Maurice was towed back, and the doctors quickly determined he was mentally disturbed. He was admitted to a mental hospital immediately."

I struggled to comprehend. "He was smiling the whole time?"

Peter shook his head, "No, he also shouted nonsensical phrases, including your name."

I leaned forward, intent on understanding every detail. "Did you notice his sailing diary? Even under duress, he kept it diligently."

Peter nodded, "Yes, I knew of his habit. It's why I brought it here, hoping to discern what he encountered."

He pulled the diary from his briefcase, handing it to me with a heavy heart.

I recognized it instantly. I had seen Captain Moore scribbling in it countless times aboard the Maurice. I flipped through the pages, skimming the uneventful entries until I reached the day of the incident.

On that day, Moore had scrawled just a single, hasty word: "Return."

The pages following were blank for several days. Then, disjointed sentences replaced the logbook entries, the writing nearly illegible: "Now I believe that anything can happen at sea!"

His handwriting, once meticulous, was now erratic. In the subsequent entries, only two words appeared over and over: "Save me."

The repeated cries for help in the diary sent chills down my spine. Captain Moore had clearly endured immense psychological torment on his return journey. He had clung to sanity for as long as possible, but eventually, his mind had succumbed to the pressure. The final, unfinished "Save me" trailed off into a long, desperate line, a haunting testament to his ultimate collapse.

I closed the diary, overwhelmed by the weight of it all, and sat in silence as the reality of the situation sank in. Recalling that fateful day, I remembered the unease that had settled over me when Moore and Mellon surfaced. It had been obvious that they were concealing something, and my anger at their secrecy had driven me away.

But now, I realized their silence had been to protect me. Whatever they encountered beneath the sea was beyond what most could bear. Mellon's suicide and Moore's madness were tragic confirmations of this. They had tried to shield me from the horror they could not articulate, a horror that had ultimately consumed them.

After a long pause, I asked, "What do the doctors say? Is there any hope for recovery?"

Mr. Moore shook his head, his voice tinged with despair. "The doctors say that with mental disorders, recovery is uncertain. But if he can be encouraged to talk about what he experienced, there might be hope. They call it 'etiology induction.'"

I grimaced. "But if he's completely mad, how can anyone hold a coherent conversation with him?"

Mr. Moore avoided my gaze, his hands fidgeting. "Yes, but perhaps the person who was with him that day could reach him."

"You mean me," I replied, understanding his implication.

He turned to me, hopeful eyes meeting mine, and nodded.

I stood up, resolved. "Alright, I'll go with you. Maybe I can help him."

Mr. Moore rose as well, grasping my hand in gratitude. "Thank you. Even if your presence doesn't help, I'm grateful for your willingness."

Touched by his sincerity, I assured him, "No need to thank me. Moore is my friend. I'm ready to leave at once."

We parted with mutual resolve, and soon, I was at the airport with Mr. Moore. During the flight, he shared more about his son, hoping to equip me with insight for our upcoming encounter.

Upon landing, company staff met us, whisking us straight to the mental hospital. Nestled on a mountainside, the hospital exuded a serene beauty. We passed verdant landscapes — lush mountains, cascading waterfalls, and vibrant springs — scenes of tranquility belied by the institution's purpose.

The hospital itself was pristine, its white walls and expansive lawns inviting. Patients, accompanied by nurses, strolled peacefully — a testament to their milder conditions. Yet, their vacant, wooden expressions were haunting reminders of the burdens they bore.

As we walked, I noticed a girl crouched before a cluster of dandelions, unmoving. Her stillness mirrored the silent suffering that pervaded the place, a poignant reminder of the fragility of the mind.

Reading the repeated cries for help in the diary was deeply unsettling. It was clear that Captain Moore had endured immense psychological torment on his return journey. He had held on as long as he could, but at some point, his mind had simply collapsed, as evidenced by the unfinished "Save me" trailing into a long, desperate line.

I closed the diary, overwhelmed by the weight of it all, and sat in silence as the reality of the situation sank in. Recalling that fateful day, I remembered the unease that had settled over me when Moore and Mellon surfaced. It had been obvious that they were concealing something, and my anger at their secrecy had driven me away.

But now, I understood that their silence had been for my protection. Whatever they encountered beneath the sea was beyond what most could bear. Mellon's suicide and Moore's madness were tragic confirmations of this.

They had tried to shield me from the horror they could not articulate, a horror that had ultimately consumed them. After a long pause, I asked, "What do the doctors say? Is there any hope for recovery?"

Mr. Moore shook his head, his voice tinged with despair. "The doctors say that with mental disorders, recovery is uncertain. But if he can be encouraged to talk about what he experienced, there might be hope. They call it 'etiology induction.'"

I grimaced. "But if he's completely mad, how can anyone hold a coherent conversation with him?"

Mr. Moore avoided my gaze, his hands fidgeting. "Yes, but perhaps the person who was with him that day could reach him."

"You mean me," I replied, understanding his implication.

He turned to me, hopeful eyes meeting mine, and nodded.

I stood up, resolved. "Alright, I'll go with you. Maybe I can help him."

Mr. Moore rose as well, grasping my hand in gratitude. "Thank you. Even if your presence doesn't help, I'm grateful for your willingness."

Touched by his sincerity, I assured him, "No need to thank me. Moore is my friend. I'm ready to leave at once."

We parted with mutual resolve, and soon, I was at the airport with Mr. Moore. During the flight, he shared more about his son, hoping to equip me with insight for our upcoming encounter.

Upon landing, company staff met us, whisking us straight to the mental hospital. Nestled on a mountainside, the hospital exuded a serene beauty. We passed verdant landscapes — lush mountains, cascading waterfalls, and vibrant springs — scenes of tranquility belied by the institution's purpose.

The hospital itself was pristine, its white walls and expansive lawns inviting. Patients, accompanied by nurses, strolled peacefully — a testament to their milder conditions. Yet, their vacant, wooden expressions were haunting reminders of the burdens they bore.

As we walked, I noticed a girl crouched before a cluster of dandelions, unmoving.

Next to the girl, a nurse stood watchfully. The girl, no older than fifteen or sixteen, had beautiful blonde hair, but the vacant expression she wore as she gazed at the dandelions tugged at my heart.

We hurried across the lawn and into the hospital building. The atmosphere inside was oppressive, a haunting contrast to the serene beauty outside. Unlike a cemetery, where the gloom stemmed from the presence of the dead, here the sense of unease arose from the living, their minds ensnared by madness. As we entered, we witnessed a distressing scene: two large men, with the expressions of worried children, fought over a scrap of paper, their cries echoing through the hall.

A doctor in a white coat approached us, shaking hands with Mr. Moore. "How is George?" Mr. Moore inquired urgently.

The doctor shook his head, casting a glance my way. Mr. Moore introduced us, explaining, "This is George's attending physician, and this is Mr. Morris. George has mentioned his name."

We shook hands, and the doctor led us to his office, where Mr. Moore briefly explained my connection to Captain Moore.

In the office, I felt a growing impatience. I wanted to see Captain Moore, to understand his condition firsthand. When I voiced this desire, the doctor frowned. "Mr. Morris, his condition is severe. He remains relatively calm when alone, but becomes quite agitated when others are present."

I insisted, "But I'm here to see him. I hope to speak with him."

The doctor considered my request. "I suggest you observe him through the door first. Our wards are equipped with observation devices. What do you think?"

Though hesitant to spy on Captain Moore, I sensed the doctor's caution stemmed from a deeper concern. Reluctantly, I agreed. "Alright, but I still hope to meet him face-to-face."

The doctor sighed. "Let's see how you feel after observing him."

I exchanged a glance with Mr. Moore, who appeared resigned. Rising, I followed the doctor down a long corridor lined with rooms. Some emitted thudding noises, others echoed with repetitive, monotonous songs that sent chills down my spine.

We stopped at a door at the corridor's end. The doctor gestured for me to look through a small peephole. Leaning closer, I peered inside.

The room was sparsely furnished, and there sat Captain Moore, slumped in a chair with a vacant stare. His once vibrant eyes now seemed lost, trapped in some inner turmoil.

Seeing Captain Moore in such a state was a shock. The once confident, cheerful man I met at the bar was now a shadow of his former self. Driven by an impulse I couldn't control, I pushed the door open and stepped inside.

As soon as I entered, his screams filled the room, a sound of pure, primal terror. He lay on the bed, eyes wide with fear, hands shaking uncontrollably. "No, no!" he cried, his voice trembling.

My heart ached for him. I tried to speak gently, "Moore, it's me!"

But my presence only heightened his distress. His screams grew sharper as I inched closer. I stopped, afraid that my approach might push him over the edge. He cowered, desperately pressing himself against the wall, as if trying to become one with it.

I sighed, attempting to reach him through familiarity. "Don't you recognize me? We were on the Maurice together, searching for the shipwreck !"

The mention of the "shipwreck" triggered another wave of panic. He buried his head in the quilt, his body trembling, sweat soaking through his shirt.

Since he couldn't see me under the quilt, I moved closer, gently touching his shoulder to reassure him.

But even that light touch startled him. He leaped up as if I'd shocked him, then lunged at me with unexpected ferocity.

His attack caught me off guard. We tumbled to the floor, and before I could react, his hands clamped around my neck, squeezing relentlessly.

My vision blurred as I gasped for air. Desperately, I clawed at his wrists, but his grip was unyielding. "You should have died long ago. You should be a few rotten bones. Why don't you die?" he muttered, his voice distorted by fear and madness.

Though his words were chilling, I had no time to ponder their meaning. My survival instinct kicked in. I released his wrists and, with considerable strength, aimed a punch at his chin.

It was a desperate move, driven by necessity. I put all my force into it, knowing that if I failed, his grip would end my life.

Chapter 5

The Undersea Monster

After delivering the punch, Captain Moore's grip on my neck loosened, and he let out another chilling scream before collapsing to the floor. The door burst open as the doctor and Mr. Moore rushed in, but I quickly signaled them to stay back.

I picked myself up, rubbing my sore neck, and watched as Captain Moore slowly regained his composure. He no longer seemed afraid or aggressive, but instead, just stared at me with an unsettling intensity.

Attempting to diffuse the tension, I forced a smile. "How about now, Captain? Can we talk?"

He continued to stare, unblinking.

I considered revealing Mellon's death but decided on a different tactic. "It's okay if you don't want to tell me," I lied. "Mellon told me everything!"

At this, Captain Moore visibly trembled. Then, unexpectedly, he burst into laughter and rushed toward me — not to attack, but to embrace me, patting my shoulders as if in some delirious camaraderie. I gently pushed him back, and he sat at the bed's edge, his laughter subsiding as he returned to a vacant stare.

"Your secret is out," I pressed. "Everyone knows it!"

He flinched but did nothing more. Sensing I was getting through, I leaned closer. "What did you see down there, at the bottom of the sea?"

His reaction was immediate and visceral. He screamed—a sound so haunting it would echo in my mind for years to come. His hands shot up to grab my face, but I was ready this time, stepping back swiftly.

In a frantic move, he grabbed the pillow, covering his face and shaking violently. I reached to pull the pillow away, but his grip was ironclad. I relented, shouting, "Moore, Mellon has already spoken! You don't need to hide your fears!"

Still, he didn't respond. For the next half-hour, I tried every argument and provocation I could think of to coax a response from him, but he remained unresponsive, clutching the pillow tightly.

Finally, the doctor intervened. "Mr. Morris, I think that's enough for now. I'm afraid he can't take much more."

Defeated, I followed the doctor out of the ward, where Mr. Moore waited. His bitter smile told me he expected the lack of progress.

We returned to the doctor's office, sinking into our seats. After a moment, the doctor spoke again. "Mr. Morris, as you've seen, your presence isn't helping him."

I nodded, frustration and sadness weighing heavily on me. Despite my best efforts, Captain Moore remained trapped in his own mind, haunted by whatever horrors he'd encountered beneath the sea. The mystery of the undersea monster, whatever it might be, continued to elude us, leaving only questions and a deep, unsettling fear of the unknown.

I lowered my head, feeling the weight of the encounter with Captain Moore pressing heavily on my heart. The strange pressure of his unspoken secret hung over me like a shroud.

After a moment's thought, I spoke up. "It's not entirely useless. At least we know there's a significant secret causing his illness. If he could share it, he might find some relief."

The doctor gave a bitter smile. "True, but it's not that simple. In cases like this, the patient isn't just stubbornly refusing to share the secret. If it were, he'd be lucid. The problem is that the trauma has left his mind blank regarding the secret. Even if he wanted to tell you, he simply can't."

Mr. Moore asked, "So, is there no way to help him?"

The doctor replied, "I've researched similar cases worldwide. There have been a few, and they were resolved."

Eagerly, I asked, "How were they cured?"

The doctor explained, "By revealing the secret in front of the patient, triggering a response that brings them back to normal."

Mr. Moore and I exchanged a glance. Whatever Captain Moore and Mellon encountered underwater, only they knew, and Mellon was no longer with us.

In that shared look, we both understood the gravity of the situation and what needed to be done.

Mr. Moore stood up, resolute. "Then I'll go. I'll return to the same place and experience it. That way, I'll know."

The doctor was visibly alarmed. "Mr. Moore, I strongly advise against this. You'd be risking your own sanity. We could end up with another patient here."

Mr. Moore's determination was evident, though his face had gone pale. Before he could argue further, the doctor added, "Given your current condition, you're likely less resilient than your son. If you were to succumb to madness, your situation could be even worse."

Mr. Moore looked dissatisfied, ready to protest, but I interjected. "I'll go."

Both the doctor and Mr. Moore turned to me, surprised. Mr. Moore's willingness was driven by paternal love, but why was I prepared to take such a risk?

In the silence that followed, Mr. Moore seemed to grapple with understanding my motivation.

Finally, he spoke softly, "I think—"

Before he could finish, I explained, "I was there with them. I need to know what happened, not just for Captain Moore's sake, but for my own peace of mind. I can't walk away from this."

The room fell silent once more, the weight of my decision settling over us. We all knew the risks, but the need for answers compelled me forward, determined to unravel the mystery of what lay beneath the sea.

The weight of my decision hung in the air as the three of us sat in silence. After a pause, Mr. Moore began, "I think—"

But I cut him off. "I don't need anyone to accompany me, Mr. Moore. You might not know this about me, but I have an affinity for the strange and unknown. No matter what they encountered in the depths, no matter how horrific it was, I can handle it."

The doctor remained silent, avoiding eye contact, while Mr. Moore rubbed his hands nervously. I continued,

"This needs to be settled. I must go because if not for the traumatic experience they endured and chose to shield me from, I might have suffered the same fate."

Mr. Moore looked at me earnestly and offered, "If you need any reward—"

I interrupted again, "I don't need a reward. What I do need is for you to provide me with all the necessary equipment for this mission."

He quickly agreed, "You can use the Maurice."

I shook my head. "No, the Maurice is too slow. I'll need a high-performance seaplane instead."

"That's absolutely no problem," Mr. Moore assured me.

I smiled, "Let's not hash out all the details here—"

I placed a reassuring hand on the doctor's shoulder. "Please take good care of Captain Moore. I'll return as soon as I can."

The doctor murmured, "May God bless you."

With that, I shrugged and left the asylum with Mr. Moore. Over the following days, I prepared meticulously for the expedition. Thanks to Mr. Moore's resources, assembling the necessary equipment was efficient and thorough. I packed essentials as well as items that might prove useful in unforeseen circumstances.

Mr. Moore arranged for a medium-sized seaplane with excellent performance capabilities. Although he insisted on accompanying me, I declined his offer. He then suggested sending a renowned diving expert, but I refused again.

He coordinated with various governments through New Zealand's channels, informing them of my flight plan to the Atlantic Ocean and requesting their support and assistance.

I took off at 2 p.m., having already tested the seaplane's water takeoffs and landings multiple times. Confident in its performance, I set a straight course, flying until midnight when I reached my first scheduled refueling stop.

The journey proceeded smoothly. By noon on the third day, I arrived at the location where the Maurice had once anchored.

Flying low, I circled the area, using scientific instruments to confirm my position. I landed near the spot where the Maurice had been anchored, ready to uncover the secrets hidden beneath the waves.

That day, as I arrived at my destination, the sky was cast in a gloomy overcast, with dark clouds looming ominously above. The sea mirrored this mood, its color deep and foreboding, like the face of someone harboring deep-seated anger.

After circling the area, I began my descent. The plane gracefully landed on the water, but as it came to a halt, I felt a sense of unease. The sea, which appeared calm from above, was actually teeming with undercurrents, causing the plane to rock violently. As I stood from my seat, I had to grip the bulkhead tightly to maintain my balance. Alone on this vast ocean, any sudden change could be catastrophic, with no one around to assist.

I opened the cabin door to assess the situation. The sea's undulating surface, accentuated by the plane's motion, resembled a massive blanket being shaken, leaving me slightly dizzy. Steeling myself, I deployed an inflatable rubber boat and carefully lowered my essential gear, piece by piece.

In that moment, I regretted declining Mr. Moore's offer of an assistant. Having someone else on board would provide not only practical assistance but also a source of comfort and encouragement to alleviate the creeping fear of isolation. But now, I was alone, and the solitude only magnified my apprehension.

Determined to press on, I reminded myself of the weather report, which assured that despite the clouds, no severe changes were expected. I estimated that I wouldn't need to remain at sea for long and aimed to uncover something significant before nightfall.

Once my equipment was ready, I donned my diving gear and descended into the boat via a rope ladder.

Aligning myself with the direction Mellon had taken on his fateful dive, I plunged into the water.

The chill of the sea took my breath away, and I shivered involuntarily as I adjusted to the temperature. Lying on the submarine propeller, I oriented myself and began my descent, following the path Mellon had taken.

As I reached the sea floor, the stark whiteness of the sand surprised me. It was fine and pristine, almost ethereal in its purity. Guiding the propeller, I moved forward cautiously. The seabed was eerily calm, indistinguishable from any other ocean floor. Yet I remained vigilant, scanning for any anomaly.

Time seemed to stretch as I completed my first circuit and began a second, broadening my search radius. By the second circuit, I estimated I was roughly 500 meters from the plane. As I embarked on the third circuit, expanding out to 800 meters, the environment remained tranquil, the only signs of life being schools of fish darting around me.

Then, in the northwest sector, I noticed something unusual. A suspicious object lay about 100 meters away. My heart quickened with anticipation as I propelled myself toward it, hoping it would provide the answers we so desperately sought.

As I approached, the outline became unmistakable—a sunken ship lay before me. My heart pounded with a mix of excitement and apprehension. Finding the wreck so quickly, within an hour of diving, felt almost too easy, adding an eerie edge to my anticipation.

The ship was partially buried in the sand, its bow protruding majestically. The seawater was clear, revealing the distinct features of a grand vessel from the Spanish Navy's golden age. Guiding the submarine propeller closer, I recognized the emblem on the bow; this was the very "ghost ship" Captain Moore had been searching for.

I imagined what must have happened that day. Mellon, diving first, would have discovered the ship and reported back to Captain Moore. Meanwhile, I had been asleep on deck. For reasons unknown, Captain Moore didn't wake me but instead joined Mellon in the water.

Yet, what transpired next? What horrors did they encounter that drove them to surface in such terror, with one ending his life and the other losing his sanity?

Now, here I was, staring at the same ship, poised to uncover the mystery that had shattered their lives. Despite the tension knotting in my stomach, I pressed on, reaching out to touch the hull.

A strange sensation coursed through me. Though the ship had supposedly lain here for centuries, the wood felt remarkably intact, solid and well-preserved, as if it had sunk mere hours ago.

Securing the propeller beside the ship, I "climbed" or rather "ascended" along the hull to reach the deck. The ship was tilted at a 45-degree angle, with its stern buried in the seabed's fine, white sand.

Stepping onto the deck, my astonishment deepened. From every angle, this appeared not as a centuries-old wreck, but as a ship in pristine condition. The navigational equipment, the ropes, the rails — all looked new, untouched by time or decay.

The sense of doubt gnawed at me as I tried to make sense of the bizarre reality before me. The ship, supposedly submerged for centuries, appeared eerily well-preserved, and the emptiness of the cabin only added to my confusion. My heart raced, and I had to remind myself to breathe steadily, to keep calm despite the surreal circumstances.

Reaching the door, I gently pulled it open. It drifted outward, revealing a dark interior. I hesitated, then swam inside, switching on my light.

The beam illuminated a spacious cabin. Nothing. Just a stark, bare space, devoid of the expected artifacts or clues. Yet, the wooden carvings on the windows were remarkably detailed and pristine, as if crafted recently. It was as though time had bypassed this ship, leaving it untouched by decay.

In any other scenario, I might have shouted, "Is there anyone here?" But in the oppressive silence of the depths, I held my tongue. My heart thundered in my chest, each beat a reminder of the uncanny reality I faced. I was indeed inside a sunken ship—a vessel that should have been a decaying relic of the past. Yet here it was, pristine and enigmatic, defying the passage of time.

I swam through the cabin, preparing to explore the ship further, when a sound pierced the watery silence—a rhythmic "pat pat pat" emanating from below.

The noise sent a chill through me, as if I'd plunged into icy waters. I froze, my breath caught in my throat. The sound was unmistakable, like the deliberate hammering of a nail.

This wasn't the first time I'd heard it. On that fateful day, as I awoke on the deck of the Maurice, I had heard it through the static of an abandoned radio intercom.

Now, the sound resonated more vividly, echoing through the hull. I inhaled sharply, steeling myself, and swam out of the cabin.

Once outside, the noise grew clearer, more insistent. I could pinpoint its origin—it was coming from the stern, from the part of the ship buried deep in the sea's sandy embrace.

Driven by a mix of dread and curiosity, I knew I had to uncover the source of this haunting sound, to delve deeper into the mystery that had claimed Captain Moore and Mell0n.

A ship that has been submerged for centuries, with most of it buried beneath the sand, shouldn't be making any sound—let alone the persistent hammering of nails.

I felt my resolve wavering, courage slipping away as the strangeness of the situation overwhelmed me. The instinct to flee, to surface and return to the safety of the plane, was nearly overpowering.

But I had come here with a purpose. I had vowed to uncover whatever mystery lay beneath the waves, to honor Captain Moore's legacy. It was easy to make bold promises on dry land, but confronting the unknown was an entirely different challenge.

Clutching the side of the boat, I was poised to push off and escape this eerie wreck when something caught my eye: a small radio walkie-talkie.

It lay wedged between two wooden posts near the cabin, undoubtedly left behind by Mellon. The sounds I had heard through the Maurice's intercom must have originated from this device.

The sight of the radio did little to bolster my courage; instead, it heightened my fear. Yet, it also ignited my curiosity, compelling me to stay and explore further.

I reached out, retrieving the radio, while the hammering continued incessantly. Nearby, I noticed a half-open hatch leading into the ship's interior. Strangely, the sea sand seemed only to envelop the ship's exterior, leaving the hull surprisingly intact.

Logic dictated that a vessel submerged for so long would be filled with sand, every crevice and gap choked with silt. Yet, given the ship's uncanny preservation, perhaps it wasn't so bizarre that the stern cabin remained untouched.

Summoning my resolve, I entered through the hatch and began a slow descent into the depths of the ship.

I swam through one cabin after another, each as empty as the last. The "pat pat" sound grew louder, more insistent, and my anxiety escalated with every stroke.

Desperately, I theorized that a large fish might have become trapped inside, throwing itself against the walls in a bid for freedom.

Driven by a mix of dread and determination, I pressed on, resolved to uncover the source of this inexplicable noise and the secrets hidden within this ghostly vessel.

Even as I clung to the notion of a trapped fish, I knew it was implausible. The sound was too precise, too rhythmic. It was unmistakably the sound of someone hammering nails.

I found myself at the door of another cabin, convinced the sound was coming from within. My heart pounded as I reached out, my hand trembling in the water—a first in my exploration career. The light on my helmet illuminated the door, revealing its structure. It was an ordinary door, reinforced with cross-shaped copper hoops, hinting that it might be the captain's quarters.

I pushed, but the door remained stubbornly closed. Frustration mingled with determination as I braced my knee against it, striking with force.

The resulting sound echoed through the water, but the hammering ceased abruptly. Silence enveloped me— a silence far more unnerving than the incessant knocking had been.

Determined, I retreated slightly and hurled myself at the door, expecting resistance. But just as I was about to collide, the hatch swung open, and I plunged inside, propelled by the ship's 45-degree tilt.

I collided with the opposite bulkhead, quickly turning to face the cabin. What I saw defied belief.

In the dim light, stood a person—not a fish, but a human being. He wore no diving gear, just simple garments reminiscent of a bygone era. His hair floated around him, and his wide eyes locked onto mine. Before him was a large wooden box, and in his hand, a hammer.

He was hammering nails into the box.

On land, such an act would be mundane, unremarkable. But here, at the bottom of the ocean, inside a ship lost for centuries, it was surreal. I remember screaming, bubbles escaping my mouth as the man swung the hammer towards me.

His first strike shattered the light on my helmet, plunging me into darkness.

Paralyzed by fear, I felt each subsequent blow, cushioned by the water's resistance but relentless nonetheless. The hammer rained down, and though the strikes weren't lethal, they sapped my strength.

Finally, I mustered enough resolve to push him away. I floated upward, a torrent of bubbles marking my ascent. As I breached the hatch, I quickly slammed the door shut, gasping for air.

The dim, watery world beneath the sea had swallowed me whole. Driven by raw instinct, a primal response to the fear gnawing at my sanity, I scrambled for safety. My mind, once a fortress of rational thought, was now a fragile, crumbling ruin. The details of my frenzied escape were a blur, lost in the whirlwind of adrenaline and terror. I moved like a cornered animal, desperate and relentless, pushing against the door with a force I couldn't comprehend. How long had I kept pushing? Time had lost its meaning as I fought to break free.

After what seemed like an eternity, I ascended again. My limbs, propelled by sheer desperation, carried me upwards. Each movement was a frantic grasp for survival. The enigma of how I escaped from the ship remained an unreadable chapter in a book I couldn't revisit. Drawn to a distant light, a beacon in the dark abyss, I swam with every ounce of determination, knowing my life hung by a thread. How far I swam, I couldn' t tell. But when my head finally broke the surface of the sea, salvation awaited in the form of a seaplane, its silhouette a promise of safety not far from where I emerged.

The moment my head breached the water, disbelief washed over me. Was this real, or a cruel mirage spun by the depths to mock my survival? With renewed vigor, I propelled myself toward the seaplane, grasping the ladder that dangled from its hatch as if it were a lifeline to reality.

I tore off the hood, lungs burning. The hood drifted on the water, its embedded light shattered. If everything I encountered at the bottom of the sea was an illusion, would the light on the hood break along with the illusion?

I tried to calm myself, panting heavily, and descended a few more rungs ladder. With shaking hands, I retrieved the hood from the sea, clambered into the cabin, and dared to look again. I needed to be inside, to feel the solid presence of the plane beneath me, before confronting the truth of what I' d seen. If everything below had been real, if the light and the fear were not mere phantoms, I feared I'd be unable to hold on, the sea ready to reclaim me.

Settled inside, I dared to inspect the hood once more. The light was indeed shattered, and the aluminum bore concave marks, imprints of violence. It was as if a hammer had been wielded against it with malice.

A vision of a man at the ocean's floor, hammer in hand, flashed before me—a specter that made my head throb anew with remembered pain. Horror gripped me again, and my body, drained of strength, went limp. All I could manage was to draw breath, each one a triumph over the terror that still clung to me.

I don't recall how long I sat paralyzed in that seat, lost to the world. The encroaching darkness outside was my only clue—a silent witness to the hours spent in a daze, my mind as blank as a slate, my body as unresponsive as a marionette with severed strings.

Then, a sudden jolt, like a needle's prick, snapped me back to reality. I sprang up, slamming the cabin door shut with urgency born of panic. My hands, trembling with residual fear, fumbled with the engine controls.

Overwhelmed by panic, my entire body trembled uncontrollably. The seaplane charged across the water's surface for what felt like an eternity—thirty minutes of mindless motion—before I realized I had forgotten to engage the takeoff lever.

Once airborne, my breaths came in ragged gasps as I frantically reached out to the nearest airport, my words tumbling over themselves in a frantic request for an emergency landing.

The seaplane itself was mechanically sound; the problem lay with me, the pilot. My skills, normally sufficient for such a craft, were compromised by the tremors that wracked my body, more violent than those of a fevered patient. All I craved was the solace of solid ground beneath me.

The airport's response was a blur, lost to my ears, yet some shred of survival instinct guided me toward the destination.

The landing was a testament to my unraveling state— a violent bounce on the runway, the plane shuddering as one wing gave way. Emergency sirens wailed in the distance, a cacophony of chaos that barely registered as my consciousness slipped away.

When Captain Mellon and Captain Moore emerged from the water that day, their faces mirrored the horror I felt, yet they remained conscious. It wasn't a question of their nerves being stronger than mine; rather, it was the strength found in numbers. They had each other, and they saw me as soon as they surfaced.

When fear grips you, its tendrils wrap tightly around your mind, squeezing rational thought into submission. Alone, that fear magnifies, becoming an unbearable weight. But the presence of others can diffuse it, offering the mind a lifeline back to sanity.

I had no such lifeline. Solitude compounded my terror until I succumbed to it entirely, fainting the moment I landed, without ever seeing another soul.

Nine days later, a psychiatrist shared his insights. He explained that fainting in response to overwhelming fear can be a blessing in disguise. It offers the nerves a much-needed respite, a chance to reset. Without this unconscious interlude, the mind risks spiraling into madness.

When I finally awoke, I found myself in a hospital room. A doctor stood vigil at my bedside, and as I stirred, he leaned in, his voice a calm anchor. "You've been through a lot," he said. "I've given you a sedative. Rest is what you need now."

I blinked, attempting to rise, but he gently pressed me back, his gaze locking with mine. Whether it was the sedative or some unspoken command in his eyes, I couldn't tell. My body, exhausted beyond words, surrendered to his suggestion. My eyes fluttered shut, and I drifted back into the soothing embrace of sleep, the world and its terrors fading to black.

Chapter 6

The Attack of the Ghost Ship

I awoke after an unbroken, twenty-hour slumber, feeling as if my mind and body had finally realigned. The nurse's gentle touch helped me rise, and after a refreshing shower and a rejuvenating meal, I felt my spirits lift. Though the memories of the ocean's depths still haunted me, they no longer held the same paralyzing terror. Past encounters with the bizarre and absurd had fortified me for such moments.

Then, Mr. Moore arrived.

He burst into the ward with an air of urgency. "As soon as I heard about your emergency landing, I came straight away. How are you holding up?"

I mustered a smile. "I'm alright, though the plane didn't fare as well."

He dismissed my concern with a wave of his hand. "Forget the plane. I need to know what happened down there."

I took a moment to gather my thoughts. "Please, listen calmly and trust every word I say."

Mr. Moore's demeanor shifted, his expression growing grave as I recounted my underwater ordeal. With each detail, his face grew more troubled, until finally, he stood in silence.

"You think—" I began, but he cut me off abruptly. "If I'd known this was going to happen, I never would have let you dive."

His words stunned me, and anger flared within. "You don't believe me at all, do you?"

His tone softened slightly, the conflict evident in his eyes. "It's not that I don't believe you. It's just... decades of education make it hard to accept your account as reality. I can only believe—"

I pressed him, my frustration boiling over, "Believe what? Tell me!"

Despite my agitation, Mr. Moore maintained his composure. "Sir, it's all hallucinations. Diving that deep can cause the mind to see things that aren't there."

I retorted, "I wish they were illusions, but the evidence is real—the light on my hood was shattered, and there were dents from a hammer. Hallucinations don't leave tangible marks."

He countered quickly, "When in the throes of hallucinations, you might have thrashed about, damaging the hood against something hard."

I sighed, "It wasn't me hitting something hard. It was a hammer in the hand of a man!"

Mr. Moore's stare was piercing, unsettling. Anger surged, and I leapt to my feet, shouting, "Don't look at me like I'm insane!"

My outburst jolted him, and in that instant, I understood — he truly thought I might be mad. His reaction confirmed it, and a heavy silence fell between us, awkward and suffocating. We were two men standing at the crossroads of belief and disbelief, trapped in the uncomfortable stillness of doubt.

After a prolonged silence, Mr. Moore finally spoke, his voice heavy with resignation. "Mr. Morris, what is it you expect of me?"

I met his unwavering gaze. "First, I want to visit your son at the mental hospital. I need to talk to him face to face. Second, I hope you can leverage your resources to form an underwater search team, to uncover and reveal the truth of this mystery."

Mr. Moore listened, a bitter smile tugging at his lips. "I'm sorry, but I can't grant either of those requests."

His refusal struck me like a physical blow. I struggled to find my voice, the words tumbling out slowly. "You won't even let me see him again?"

He shook his head, his expression pained. "It's not that I won't let you see him, but..." His voice trailed off, his face etched with sorrow that deepened the lines across his brow. Seeing him like this filled me with dread. "He...Captain... what happened to him?" I asked, my voice barely above a whisper.

Mr. Moore turned away, his back a rigid shield against his grief, yet his voice betrayed him. "The day after you left, a nurse came in to bring him food. He panicked and attacked her. In self-defense, she struck him with a bottle. When help arrived, he was already gravely injured. A few hours later, he... passed away."

Stunned, I found myself speechless. All my efforts, all the risks I'd taken, had been for nothing. The truth that might have saved him came too late.

Mr. Moore turned back to me, his movements slow and deliberate. "Consider it a nightmare," he said, his voice hollow.

I had no words of comfort to offer. Mr. Moore had suffered a loss so profound that any attempt at consolation felt futile. I placed a hand on his shoulder, searching for words that might bridge the chasm between us. "Mr. Moore, for you, this may seem like a nightmare. But for me, it's a mystery that needs solving. I want to clear your son's name, to prove he was a skilled navigator, not a victim of hallucinations at sea."

His silence stretched between us, heavy and contemplative.

"This was his greatest concern in life," I continued. "His reputation. A man's life may end, but his honor should endure."

Mr. Moore sighed deeply, a sound heavy with unspoken understanding. I added softly, "I'll pursue this on my own. I won't trouble you further."

He sighed again, his voice barely above a whisper. "I understand your intentions, but I wish you could simply rest and let it go."

Despite my best efforts, I couldn't muster a smile. Instead, my expression mirrored my resolve. I didn't agree with his wish to forget, but I didn't need to say it aloud; it was written across my face.

Mr. Moore wiped a hand across his weary features. "Medicine may be advanced, but it can't erase memories. If only it could, perhaps I'd choose to forget I ever had a son. It would make life easier to bear."

His words hung in the air, a testament to the depth of his grief and the burden of memory that we both carried.

I fixed my gaze on him. "Why won't you even consider what I saw in the sea?"

Mr. Moore shook his head, a gesture of weary dismissal. I paced the room, desperate for a solution. "What if you and I dive together, armed and equipped with cameras? We could capture the man in the water, or even bring him back alive."

He looked at me, his eyes reflecting a fatigue that went beyond physical exhaustion. "Mr. Morris, you should rest."

Despite my impassioned words, I realized he didn't believe me. The weight of his grief had sapped his will to act. I lay back on the bed, and he sighed. "I'm so sorry. I'm just too tired, too weary to do anything."

There was nothing more to say. His sorrow was a barrier I couldn't breach, and I couldn't force him into action. We sat in silence, an unspoken understanding passing between us, until he finally said, "I'm leaving. I wish you good luck."

I managed a bitter smile and walked with him through the hospital's long corridors. We didn't speak, but the silence felt less like a parting and more like a shared burden.

At the hospital entrance, we shook hands, and he turned to leave. But just as he was about to get into his car, he hesitated and returned to me with urgency.

"There's something I should tell you," he said.

His mention of Captain Moore's death signaled that this was important. I listened intently.

"It's strange," he began, "my son died from a severe blow to the head—"

His voice carried the weight of something significant. "In the last ten seconds of his life, he was completely lucid. When he woke from his coma, he wasn't mad."

I nodded, understanding the gravity of his words. "A miracle, perhaps. His mind cleared, even if just briefly."

Mr. Moore continued, "Yes, but it was so brief—only ten seconds before his heart stopped."

I leaned in, my breath quickening. "Did he say anything during those final moments? How did you know he was lucid?"

He nodded. "He spoke. I was there, along with several doctors. He recognized me, called me father, and said the man hit him hard. He knew he wouldn't survive. I didn't even have the chance to explain that the nurse acted in self-defense before he passed."

The revelation left me breathless. "Did he mention someone hitting his head?"

Mr. Moore confirmed, "Yes, the nurse struck him."

I paused, considering his words. "Mr. Moore, I believe his last words weren't about the nurse. I think he was recalling the attack under the sea, the man with the hammer."

His demeanor changed, his voice stern. "Mr. Morris, in his final moments, my son was clear-minded. He knew who I was."

With that, Mr. Moore turned sharply, retreating to his car. He drove away, leaving me standing there, grappling with the unresolved tension between belief and disbelief, and the haunting mystery of the ghost ship.

Captain Moore's final words echoed in my mind, dispelling any lingering doubt. Everything I had encountered beneath the sea was real, not a figment of a troubled mind. His words, seemingly about the nurse, were, to me, a confirmation of something far more sinister.

In those fleeting moments of clarity before his death, Captain Moore had glimpsed a truth buried deep in his past — a truth from before his mind succumbed to madness. Medically, it made sense; his memory would revert to events prior to his mental disorder. Someone, or something, had struck him hard before his descent into chaos.

There was no question in my mind: Captain Moore had been attacked by the same mysterious figure I encountered, a man living impossibly in the watery grave of the sunken ship.

Chilled to the bone, I finally moved, the cold night air driving me back to the ward. The reality of a person dwelling in the depths was astonishing, yet undeniably true.

Though only three of us had seen him, and two were now dead, I was determined to reveal this underwater enigma to the world.

I knew the path forward. If others dismissed my claims, I would gather the proof myself. Equipped with an underwater camera, I would capture the elusive inhabitant of the shipwreck, bringing irrefutable evidence to light.

Resolved, I left the hospital, relocating to a nearby hotel. I reached out to my family, requesting the funds necessary for my venture. Within three days, everything was in place: a reliable boat and all the gear I needed for another dive.

As I set sail, the sun dipped below the horizon, and darkness enveloped the sea. I decided to wait until morning to dive. The night was calm, the moon casting a silvery glow across the water. The boat rocked gently, lulled by the rhythmic embrace of the waves. Sleep eluded me, the adrenaline of my impending mission coursing through my veins.

By midnight, still restless, I donned a coat and stepped onto the deck. A thickening fog rolled in, blanketing the sea in a cool, damp shroud. I sat down, lighting a cigarette, listening to the soft sizzle as the moisture in the air mingled with the burning tobacco.

The fog hung heavy over the sea, a harbinger of a clear day to come once it lifted at sunrise. This was ideal for my dive. I had calculated the coordinates meticulously, and my boat was anchored no more than fifty meters from the sunken ship. The thought of capturing evidence with my camera, revealing the mysterious inhabitant of the wreck, set my heart racing and chased away any trace of sleep.

I smoked through a trio of cigarettes, their embers glowing in the mist, when a peculiar "bobo" sound caught my attention. It was unmistakable — something was moving through the water, disturbing the surface with rhythmic splashes.

I stood, straining to judge the sound's proximity. It seemed to be all around me, yet the dense fog obscured everything beyond a shroud of white.

Panic surged through me as the eerie, familiar sound resonated through the thick fog. Memories flooded back of that night aboard the "Maurice" when Captain Moore had roused Mellon and me to the same haunting noises. Back then, the sounds were distant, but now they were disturbingly close, enveloping me from every direction.

I spun around, my voice breaking the silence as I shouted into the void, "Who is it?" My cries echoed futilely into the mist, the splashing sounds drawing nearer with each passing moment.

Then, it emerged—a ghostly specter of an ancient sailing ship, bearing down on my vessel with alarming speed. The fog parted just enough to reveal its imposing form, a mere thirty meters away. I stood frozen, disbelief rooting me to the deck as the ship's prow and tall mast came into sharp, undeniable focus.

A chilling laugh pierced the air, and my eyes locked onto a figure on the bow. He lounged carelessly atop a pile of ropes, mouth twisted into a sinister grin. Recognition hit me like a jolt of electricity—this was the man from the sunken ship, the one who had wielded a hammer against me.

Reeling back, I stumbled toward the hatch, only to glimpse two more ships emerging from the fog, flanking me on either side. Each bore the emblem of a sea monster, coiled menacingly around the bow.

Three ghost ships! A spectral fleet converging upon me.

In that moment, Captain Moore's tale of ghost ships became stark reality. These were the very vessels that had driven his ship to disaster, their lethal presence now threatening me.

My situation was dire, worse than Captain Moore's encounter with the ghost ships. He had the presence of mind to change course and evade them, but I was frozen in place, unable to act.

If I had been calm, perhaps I could have dashed to the cabin, started the engine, and steered clear of danger when the first ship loomed through the fog. But calmness eluded me.

When that first ship emerged, I was paralyzed. I stood, rooted to the spot, as it bore down on me. Only when I retreated to the cabin door did I see the other two ships closing in from either side. I was trapped in a surreal tableau, unable to move.

The three ghost ships converged on mine, their masts slicing through the mist. The man on the bow laughed, a sound that sent a chill through my bones.

My mind was paradoxically clear, yet my body refused to obey, locked in shock. I watched as the bows of the ghostly trio surged through the waves, colliding towards my boat.

In the midst of the chaos, a bizarre thought slipped into my mind—a desperate hope that the three ships were nothing more than phantoms. Ghost ships, after all, were supposed to be mere illusions, spectral shadows that couldn't exert any real force. As they barreled toward my vessel with such ferocity, I clung to the notion that they would pass harmlessly through, like mist through a sieve, leaving me unscathed and proving my fears unfounded.

It was a comforting thought, albeit a ridiculous one, born of desperation and the intense pressure of the moment. My rational mind, usually grounded in science and logic, had reached a breaking point, grasping at the implausible to shield me from the terrifying reality.

But as the ships closed in, the illusion shattered. They didn't pass through as I had fervently hoped. Instead, their collision was all too real, the "crunch" of wood and metal unmistakable as my boat was caught and crushed between them. The reality of ghost ships became undeniable in that instant, their spectral nature giving way to devastating substance, leaving me with only enough time to scream before everything went dark.

I have no sense of how much time had passed before I gradually returned to consciousness. The first sensation was a persistent buzzing, a murmur of voices I couldn't quite decipher. My eyes remained shut, and an overwhelming, primal fear coursed through me. It was as if I were back at sea, enveloped in the suffocating fog, the memory of the ghost ships crashing toward me vivid and terrifying.

In my mind's eye, I could see the emblems on the ships and the man with the eerie smile. The fear was visceral, a desperate urge to hide, to escape from the spectral menace that haunted my thoughts.

Suddenly, a pressure on my shoulder jolted me, prompting a scream as my eyes flew open. The room was filled with people, their faces a blur in the brightness that seemed to assault my senses. The light felt intrusive, unbearable, and I craved the safety of darkness, the only refuge where I could conceal myself.

In a panic, I shoved the person nearest to me and bolted forward, colliding with obstacles, hearing raised voices all around. My flight was halted abruptly when I collided with something immovable. Still, the darkness eluded me, so I pressed my hands over my eyes, seeking the comfort of shadow in my self-imposed blindness.

Yet the fear persisted, accompanied by the sensation of being ensnared, as if the monstrous beings from the ship emblems had come to life, their tentacles binding me with relentless force. I fought back with every ounce of strength, resisting the imagined pull toward the ocean depths, where I knew I couldn't survive. I was of the land; they belonged to the sea.

The struggle was fierce, and at moments, I felt a fleeting release before being entrapped again by stronger forces. My screams and thrashing continued until exhaustion claimed me, and consciousness slipped away once more, leaving me in merciful oblivion.

Chapter 7

Flora's Diary

At this point, I must introduce a segment from Flora's diary. The reasons for this will become clear as you continue reading. The diary chronicles events day by day, each entry capturing the unfolding reality. Naturally, in these entries, the first-person "I" refers to Flora.

* * *

He woke up!

I stood there, staring at him, a profound sadness welling up inside me. I wanted to cry, to release the anguish, but the tears wouldn't come. My grief was so overwhelming that it rendered me almost immobile.

He had endured so much, faced so many trials, yet the thought of him succumbing to madness had never crossed my mind.

I don't know the cause of his breakdown. All I know is that nine days ago, he requested a significant sum of money, without explaining why.

When I finally saw him, it was already the third day after he had been admitted to the mental hospital.

They—an old cargo ship—had found him adrift in the Atlantic, clinging to a large piece of wood, unconscious. They rescued him, but he attacked the crew in a fit of panic. In response, they restrained him, knocked him out, and brought him here.

Fortunately, his notebook survived the ordeal, allowing us to confirm his identity. But no one could unravel the mystery of what he had encountered at sea. The doctors said there was no hope for his recovery. Yet, I refuse to believe that. Even though he no longer recognizes me, his own wife, I cling to the belief that there is hope.

* * *

He remains unchanged. It's too painful to face him directly, so I watch him through the small window in the door, as he reacts fearfully to anyone who approaches, even me.

What terrifies him so? What is the source of his fear?

I watched him eat, and it was heart-wrenching. He seemed more animal than human, clutching his eyes with one hand while shoving food into his mouth with the other. It was brutal to witness. How did it come to this? Why did this happen to my husband, to us?

* * *

Today, for the first time, I allowed myself to cry.

The tears finally came when I met with a Mr. Moore, who offered me words of comfort and encouraged me to be brave in the face of this harsh reality. I'd been holding back my tears for days, but once they started, they flowed uncontrollably.

I knew that my husband had met a New Zealand captain named Moore. This Mr. Moore was the captain's father. He shared many things with me that seemed beyond belief.

Yet, deep down, I sensed that Mr. Moore's words were true. He explained that his son's condition mirrored my husband's current state. Both were driven to madness by terrifying, unknown events at sea, events so haunting that even a renowned expert had taken his own life.

Though I struggled to accept it, I couldn't deny the reality that my husband had lost his mind. The doctor attributed it to overwhelming fear and trauma. Mr. Moore insisted it was connected to a ghost ship and a mysterious figure living underwater, someone he claimed to have seen in a sunken ship.

I'm at a loss. Who can help me? Who can possibly offer us a way out?

***

Mr. Moore visited me daily, despite his extensive business commitments in New Zealand. His concern for Ash was genuine and unwavering. Yet, Ash showed no signs of improvement. My tears seemed endless, but even they brought no change.

Perhaps crying isn't the answer. Perhaps I need to take action, or at the very least, remain calm. Ash had faced many harrowing experiences before, but this time, it seemed different. Could he truly be insane?

Should I venture to that place and see for myself?

***

Yesterday, I shared my thoughts with Mr. Moore. He was a man of direct words. He chastised me as if I were a child, urging me to abandon such a reckless idea that could only exacerbate the situation.

I didn't argue with him, though we viewed the matter through different lenses. To him, the situation could deteriorate further; to me, it had already reached rock bottom.

I believe it's time for me to decide my next steps.

* * *

Flora's Diary (continued)

My brother, fresh from a dam project in India, rushed over as soon as he heard the news. He believed his presence might help Ash, and I, fighting back tears, took him to see Ash. But Ash's reaction was alarming. His entire body trembled, and the veins on his forehead bulged with strain. I quickly pulled brother aside and explained everything that had happened.

Initially, I hesitated to share the full story, knowing brother's temperament. He was the kind of person who, once aware of a situation, would plunge headfirst into danger without a second thought. True to form, he began shouting halfway through my account, and by the end, he was adamant about investigating the ghost ships himself.

I had already resolved to go. My brother wasn't aware of my decision, as I hadn't disclosed it to him. Instead, I urged him not to go, emphasizing the peril and unpredictability of the situation. If Ash, with his resilience, had succumbed to madness, what chance did we have? The likelihood of both of us returning as madmen was too great.

Yet, I might have made a mistake by telling my brother everything. Now, there was no stopping him. Had I done the right thing, or was this a grave error?

* * *

Mr. Moore reprimanded me once again and clashed with my brother. My brother accused him of cowardice, while Mr. Moore labeled him impulsive. I had always known Mr. Moore as a composed and courteous gentleman, so it was surprising to see him so agitated.

His anger stemmed from genuine concern for us, but my brother and I were resolute. It dawned on me how similar our temperaments were — once we made a decision, it was nearly impossible to sway us.

* * *

Early this morning, Mr. Moore visited again. We began preparing for our journey, but crucially, we needed detailed information: the site where Captain Moore first encountered the ghost ship, the precise location of the "Maurice" when it anchored, and more. Only Mr. Moore could provide these details, since Ash was in no condition to do so.

However, Mr. Moore flatly refused. His stance was clear: he would not be complicit in leading two more people to potential doom, especially when one was the wife of a man who had faced misfortune helping his son.

My brother's temper flared again, but his frustration was understandable. This was our only lead to possibly saving Ash, much like Ash's own attempt to save Captain Moore.

Their argument escalated rapidly, turning physical when Mr. Moore threw the first punch. My brother retaliated with such force that Mr. Moore staggered back, colliding with the wall before crumpling to the ground.

Despite the blow, Mr. Moore didn't lose consciousness. Dazed, he touched his head, stood up shakily, and with an unexpectedly fervent expression, addressed us. "I never told you about my son's condition before he died, did I?"

My brother and I exchanged confused glances, unsure of his implication.

Before we could process his words, Mr. Moore revealed that Captain Moore had regained consciousness for half a minute before his death.

We were still puzzled by the significance of this.

Mr. Moore continued, "The hospital tried everything, but there's one thing they haven't tried: hitting his head."

My brother, shocked, exclaimed, "You'd risk his life for a mere half-minute of clarity?"

Mr. Moore winced as if in pain. "The nurse struck my son in self-defense, but a controlled blow might restore his sanity, even temporarily."

My brother looked at me, and I took a deep, steadying breath.

"At least," Mr. Moore urged, "we can discuss this with a doctor."

Neither my brother nor I spoke, left to ponder the desperate measure suggested by a desperate father.

* * *

The doctor paced the office anxiously, making circle after circle as my brother, Mr. Moore, and I watched in tense silence. We were on edge, fearing that he might reject our desperate plan, which felt like our last hope.

Finally, the doctor stopped and adjusted his glasses. "There are rare cases where people have fully recovered after a sudden impact. However, there is no established medical procedure for this." He paused, looking at us seriously. "This is a risky proposition. A normal person could suffer severe injury from a blow to the head. How do you propose to control the force to ensure he's not harmed further but somehow restored?"

My brother, unable to contain his urgency, shouted, "We don't have a way, but do you have any method to bring him back to normal?"

The doctor shook his head slowly, a gesture heavy with the weight of hopelessness. "I don't."

"Then let us try!" my brother insisted.

The doctor replied, "In the hospital, I cannot permit such an attempt. Outside of here, however, I bear no responsibility."

His meaning was clear: the hospital wouldn't condone it, but outside its walls, we could proceed as we saw fit. Mr. Moore and my brother decided immediately. In unison, they said, "Okay, let's move him out of the hospital!"

* * *

Moving Ash out proved far more challenging than anticipated. Our initial attempts to escort him calmly failed as he resisted violently upon seeing anyone approach. His strength was formidable, and despite the efforts of five or six male nurses, he broke free repeatedly. Ultimately, my brother restrained him long enough for the doctor to administer a sedative.

But just as the doctor moved in, Ash kicked him away and bolted, sending the hospital into chaos. He darted through the corridors, and my brother and I pursued him desperately. He burst through the hospital doors, knocking down anyone in his path.

My brother chased him relentlessly, finally tackling him just beyond the garden. As they hit the ground, the sickening "bang" of Ash's head striking a stone slab echoed sharply.

The sound was so jarring that my legs gave out beneath me, and I collapsed, certain that the impact had caused irreparable damage.

As I lay there, catching my breath, my brother rose, and I saw Ash lying still. Then, miraculously, he opened his eyes, focusing on me. "Flora!" he called out.

In that moment, hearing him recognize me and say my name, I felt a happiness and relief unlike any I had ever known, despite having heard him call my name countless times before.

I was overwhelmed, unable to find words, and tears flowed freely.

Chapter 8

Exploration Fails

Flora's diary concludes here, providing insight into a time when I was lost in madness, confined within a mental asylum. During those ten days, my mind was a whirlwind of chaos—incapable of coherent thought, my existence reduced to raw fear, screams, and struggle.

The first flicker of awareness came upon seeing Flora. Despite the blankness in my mind, I recognized her immediately. She was on the ground, overwhelmed with tears, and it dawned on me that I, too, was on the ground. Figures in white rushed towards me, and amidst the confusion, I spotted Oliver, Flora's brother, whom I hadn't seen in years. Mr. Moore was there as well, catching his breath.

Once more, I called out, "Flora!"

But Flora only cried harder, her tears an unstoppable torrent. As I stood, Oliver helped his sister to her feet, and a crowd gathered around us. I glanced at them, then down at myself, and finally at the building and its sign overhead.

In that moment, clarity struck with a chilling realization: "Was I... Am I a lunatic? Was I a lunatic?"

Oliver exclaimed something, though I couldn't discern if it was joy or surprise. He rushed to me, gripping my arm firmly, as if to anchor me, fearing I might slip away again. His strength was palpable, his fingers pressing hard into my skin. Between breaths, he managed to say, "You, you—"

Twice he repeated "you," unable to finish his thought. I placed my hand on his reassuringly and asked, "Oliver, was I really insane before? And now... am I suddenly better?"

Oliver's excitement rendered him speechless, his head bobbing in a fervent nod.

Without hesitation, I pushed past him, my focus solely on Flora, who was struggling to stand. As I reached her, she flung herself into my arms, clutching me with an intensity that spoke of desperation and relief. Her tears soaked through my white shirt, a testament to the emotional storm we had weathered.

The scene must have been quite moving, as those gathered around us were visibly affected. Some were openly weeping, their emotions mirroring the joy and relief of our reunion.

Gently, I patted Flora's arm. "It's all right now," I assured her. "Even if I was lost to madness, that's behind us."

Flora clung tightly to me, her tear-streaked face filled with a mix of relief and sorrow. Despite her haggard and thin appearance, I recognized her at first glance, though it was remarkable how much she had changed, a shadow of her former self.

"I'm not crying from sadness," she said, her voice breaking slightly. "It's joy, sheer joy!"

Oliver joined us, his voice filled with admiration. "She's been the bravest through it all. While you were gone, she stood strong. Now, let her bask in this happiness."

Though my awareness of my surroundings had returned, my mind felt muddled, struggling to recall the chain of events that led to my madness. My expression must have betrayed my inner turmoil, as two doctors approached. The elder, his hair a distinguished silver, spoke with reverence. "Thank God, truly a miracle. You need rest, and a thorough examination."

I simply nodded, acknowledging the wisdom in his words. The fatigue was bone-deep; rest was not just a suggestion but a necessity.

I remained in the mental hospital for another seven days.

By the second day, clarity returned, my mind piecing together the fragments of my ordeal. While the time lost to madness was a blur, Flora and Oliver filled in the gaps. Their accounts revealed that my experiences mirrored those of Captain Moore, a chilling parallel in our shared descent into and emergence from the abyss.

The morning after I regained full consciousness, Mr. Moore prepared to leave. As he clasped my hand firmly, his emotions were palpable. I was deeply grateful for his concern and support. Before departing, he offered a heartfelt plea: "Please, let it all go. Don't take unnecessary risks. It won't bring you any benefit."

His advice was genuine, rooted in the painful memory of Captain Moore's tragic fate—a wound that had left an indelible mark on his heart. He was determined to prevent any of us from enduring a similar tragedy.

Yet, I couldn't give him a definitive promise. My response was vague, a collection of non-committal words. His sighs lingered in the air as he turned and left.

The following days saw a parade of doctors conducting a myriad of tests. A team of eminent psychiatrists confirmed unanimously that I had returned to normalcy, attributing my recovery to an "appropriate concussion of the brain nerves."

This so-called "appropriate concussion" had occurred when I fell on the stone steps outside the hospital. While concussions are common, achieving an "appropriate" one is far less predictable and lies beyond human control. My sudden recovery was sheer serendipity, a one-in-ten-thousand chance among similar cases. It seemed, as the silver-haired doctor put it, a "miracle performed by God."

A week later, I walked out of the mental hospital. Oliver had secured a serene house by the sea, providing a haven for recovery.

Flora knew her brother and I would never let this matter rest. What she didn't expect was the scale of his pursuit, though I had anticipated it.

Knowing Oliver, his approach was unsurprising. He either did nothing or went all out. For this endeavor, I would have handled it quietly, perhaps inviting a few friends to form a modest expedition team.

However, Oliver's strategy was bold and unexpected. He detailed our story in a best-selling mystery magazine, publicly calling for volunteer explorers to join the search for the "centuries-old sea dweller" and the elusive "ghost ships." His article, filled with evidence validating my experiences, sparked global interest. Calls, telegrams, and letters inundated our once-quiet rented house. Within a month, the house overflowed with people, many setting up tents and temporary shelters outside.

Oliver meticulously vetted expedition candidates, spending a month selecting from the flood of applicants. Ultimately, 134 individuals, each meeting stringent criteria, were deemed fit to join the expedition. Qualifications included funding their expenses or providing essential resources like ships and helicopters. Oliver's business acumen shone brightly; he harnessed public curiosity to assemble a formidable expedition team, complete with state-of-the-art equipment and diverse talent, in just six weeks.

When the expedition finally set off, it was a grand spectacle. Naturally, Flora and I accompanied them, ready to face whatever lay ahead.

When news broke of Oliver's ambitious expedition, even Mr. Moore was taken aback by the scale of his undertaking. Yet, upon learning the details, he threw his support behind the endeavor, providing all the information he had.

Describing every member of the expedition and the myriad of events that unfolded at sea would be impossible, given the sheer number of participants. Suffice it to say, after 20 days of diligent effort, the expedition's outcome could be summed up succinctly: "disappointment."

Though the expedition spanned 20 days, the exodus of team members began on the tenth day. By the fifteenth day, fewer than half remained, and by the eighteenth day, only three of us persisted: Oliver, Flora, and myself.

With just the three of us left, our once-grand expedition had dwindled to a single boat and a handful of gear.

The steady departure of our comrades was driven by our lack of discoveries. Over twenty days, we endured several fog-shrouded nights, hoping for a glimpse of the elusive "ghost ship." Yet the fog yielded nothing—neither sight nor sound of anything beyond the mist.

Each member logged over ten dives on average, myself included, exploring the depths repeatedly.

The seabed, however, was eerily tranquil. No sign of shipwrecks, and certainly no trace of the mysterious figure rumored to dwell below, wielding a hammer. The location was precise. I recognized the familiar rocks beneath the waves, yet the ship was absent.

Oliver had been forthright with recruits, cautioning that while he believed in the possibility, he couldn't guarantee results. Thus, the departing members bore him no ill will, though I was not spared their skeptical glances.

Oliver's bold venture did stir trouble. On our return, the police scrutinized his actions for a month, probing for any hint of deceit. Thankfully, the investigation cleared him of wrongdoing, but not without causing significant headaches.

That, however, was a concern for later. As we sat in the cramped cabin, preparing to head home, Oliver and I took one last dive, clinging to hope. Again, we surfaced with nothing.

Back in the cabin, Oliver, drowning his frustrations in wine, declared, "There's nothing left to say. Perhaps it was all a grand illusion."

I replied coolly, "Blaming it all on illusion is the easy way out."

Oliver gestured in resignation. "Then—"

I cut him off sharply, "Don't ask me for answers I can't provide. But I am certain of one thing: everything I experienced was no illusion."

Despite the lack of tangible proof, my conviction remained unshaken. The mysteries of the sea lingered, hidden for now, but undeniably real.

Flora interjected, "Alright, let's not argue. What do we do now? Do we head back or continue?"

In that moment, frustration washed over me. "Of course, we should go back. What else is there to wait for?"

With a sigh, Flora agreed. We left it at that, setting a course for home. Upon reaching the shore, a crowd of reporters awaited us. Oliver faced them with open arms, declaring, "We failed. There's nothing more a loser can say!"

His bold admission was enough to disperse the reporters, allowing us to leave promptly. With Oliver returning to India, Flora and I made our way home.

During the journey, Flora avoided bringing up the expedition, and I was grateful for it. There was nothing left to say. I had replayed my encounters a thousand times, convinced they were not mere illusions.

Yet, given the futile results of our search, what could I possibly say?

Back home, my story had become a sensation. Many sought to hear it firsthand, yet over time, recounting those events became something I dreaded. A few persistent individuals, who refused to let the matter rest, found themselves at odds with me.

Months passed. Though those experiences never left me, mentions of them dwindled.

Had I not attended that party, perhaps these experiences would have remained unresolved, like countless other mysteries. But the party did happen.

Hosted by a British friend, it was attended by about twenty diplomats and international business representatives. I was drawn to the gathering by the promise of a post-dinner discussion on "aliens"—extraterrestrial visitors to Earth. Invited as the primary speaker, I was there to defend my belief in intelligent life beyond our planet.

The banquet itself was unremarkable, marked by the customary politeness of well-dressed guests.

As the final event concluded in high spirits, I found myself at the door, alongside a tall, dark-haired young man with sharp, intelligent eyes. He approached me, saying, "Mr. Morris, I'd like to have a word with you."

Caught off guard, I realized I hadn't remembered every guest's name from the host's introductions. I replied, "Of course, what would you like to discuss?"

The young man smiled, "I'm Yunlin, Yunlin Degado, from Spain."

Until he mentioned Spain, his name had made no impression on me.

Chapter 9

Hidden Historical Secrets

The moment Yunlin Degado mentioned he was from Spain, his surname struck me with the force of a needle piercing my consciousness. I was momentarily speechless, my mind racing with possibilities. He continued, "I've wanted to approach you for some time, but it seemed too absurd, too difficult to articulate. Yet, meeting you today feels like a sign that I must speak."

I nodded, understanding. "I suspect this is about my experiences in the Atlantic?"

"Exactly, Mr. Morris," Degado confirmed. "I've read Mr. Oliver Sallow's article thoroughly. He mentioned that you and Captain Moore saw a ghost ship bearing the emblem of the Degado family."

A chill coursed through me as I inhaled sharply.

Degado met my gaze, his eyes unwavering. "I am the last descendant of this ancient and fading lineage."

As we spoke, we strolled towards my car. I suggested, "I have additional information on the Degado family at my home. Would you like to see it?"

Degado shook his head. "No one knows the rise and fall of the Degado family better than I do. I'd like to invite you to my place. There's something I need to show you."

My curiosity ignited. In my research on the Degado family, I'd sensed something peculiar. This once-celebrated seafaring dynasty, prominent in Spain's naval history, seemed abruptly erased from historical records—mentioned only in passing, and even then, shrouded in ambiguity. I'd long suspected a profound secret lay hidden within its history.

History is replete with similar enigmatic tales, where the true story remains elusive. But here was a living descendant of the Degado family. Could he reveal the secrets behind this storied lineage?

At that moment, I hadn't yet connected the Degado family directly to my underwater ordeal. However, the fact that the ghost ships bore the Degado emblem intrigued me deeply.

"If it's not too much trouble, I'd be honored to visit," I replied eagerly.

Degado smiled warmly. "I've awaited this moment for a long time. Please, follow me."

I tailed his car as he led me down a tranquil road, arriving shortly at a quaint, charming house. We parked, and Degado unlocked the door with a key. "I live alone here, temporarily, for a cultural exchange program. I'll be returning soon."

Inside, the home, though temporary, was tastefully adorned. He guided me directly to his study, where we both shed our coats.

Opening a cabinet, Degado continued, "These are items I carry with me everywhere. They're the sole surviving records of our family. Once, we were celebrated for our naval prowess. But later, labeled as traitors, we were shamed and erased from history."

His words hung in the air, heavy with the weight of untold tales and forgotten glory. I sensed that whatever he was about to reveal would be significant, a key to unlocking the mystery that had so deeply entwined our fates.

I nodded thoughtfully, "Yes, I came up empty-handed when searching for any trace of the Degado family history."

Degado moved with purpose, opening an antique cabinet and extracting a small, blackened metal box. Its surface bore the unmistakable patina of age, whispering secrets of a forgotten time.

With a deft twist, he opened the box to reveal its contents: a pair of ancient metal rings cradling a collection of keys. The keys were relics themselves, relics of locks long fallen out of fashion.

Inside, a stack of papers lay dormant. Degado lifted a sheet, "Take a look at this castle," he urged.

The castle sketched on the parchment seemed to leap to life. Drawn with charcoal, the image had aged like fine wine, its edges frayed and yellowed. Perched defiantly atop a cliff, it overlooked a tumultuous sea below, its stones whispering tales of a bygone era.

The castle's depiction was vivid, the atmosphere palpable—brooding and enigmatic.

Degado gently flattened the fragile paper, "This castle was erected during the zenith of the Degado lineage."

Curiosity piqued, I inquired, "Does it still stand?"

He nodded solemnly, "Yes."

He reached out and touched the keys once more, their metallic clink echoing through the room. "These keys," he said with a hint of pride, "are the heart of the castle. They unlock its many secrets. And yes, the castle is my inheritance now."

I studied his face, and he quickly anticipated my thoughts. "Don't mistake ownership for affluence," he clarified. "If it weren't for my deep-rooted connection to my family's history, I would have let it go long ago. Maintaining a castle is a financial quagmire. The cost of keeping it from crumbling is staggering—enough to drive one into bankruptcy. Since its original master vanished, the gates have remained shut, preserving its mystery."

I furrowed my brow in curiosity, "So you've never truly explored it?"

"I tried once," Degado confessed, his voice tinged with regret. "But the decay was

overwhelming. I barely set foot inside before the desolation pushed me back out."

I nodded slowly, "Then why reveal this painting to me now?"

He hesitated, then unveiled another set of parchments, each depicting a ship!

The moment they came into view, an electric thrill shot through me.

Three ships, etched with the same meticulous artistry, each one more mysterious than the last. My pulse quickened, sensing the onset of a grand adventure veiled in layers of history, faith, and the enigmatic legacy of the Degado family.

Each of the three ships bore emblems that sent a shiver down my spine—emblems I was all too familiar with.

They were the same ships that had collided with mine on that foggy night, sending it to the depths of the sea.

My breath quickened, a reflexive response to the flood of memories. Yunlin Degado studied me intently, "Mr. Morris, these are indeed the ships you encountered."

I managed a sound—a mix of disbelief and recognition—as I pointed to one ship in particular. "That one rests on the ocean floor. I've navigated its ghostly halls, delved into its vacant cabins, and there—"

I halted, words unnecessary. Degado knew the tale, knew what haunted me from that submerged vessel.

He nodded, "These ships were the pinnacle of their era, crafted under the watchful eye of my ancestor, Ves Degado."

I drew a deep breath, and Degado continued, "Let me show you something more. Ves was an enigmatic figure. After the ships' completion, he sailed them into oblivion, never to return. Since then, our family has been branded as traitors. Officially, it was said he deceived the crown and absconded with royal treasures, but I suspect deeper motives."

I frowned, my interest not in history but in the immediate, tangible mysteries.

Sensing my detachment, Degado urged, "I need you to remain calm."

"Why?" I asked, my curiosity piqued.

He produced another document from the box, withholding its revelation. "This is a portrait," he explained, "of Ves Degado, the architect of those ships."

A nervous energy coursed through me as Degado spoke. He didn't unveil the image immediately, heightening the suspense. "I know it's improbable, but I need you to see him—to verify something."

With a flourish, he unfolded the paper.

The sight of the man in the portrait wrenched a visceral cry from my throat—a sound that tore free, unbidden. My vision swam, and I staggered, my body betraying me. Degado's hands steadied me as I turned away, refusing to face the image again, gasping for air.

The visage on the parchment was unmistakable—Ves Degado, the man who had haunted the depths of the sea. I recalled the chilling moment he swung a hammer at my head, his laughter piercing the fog as the ships bore down upon me.

Rationality insisted it was impossible, yet every fiber of my being screamed otherwise. I felt the strength drain from me, my breath shallow and ragged. "Please, put that portrait away," I urged, my voice barely above a whisper.

Degado's curiosity was palpable. "Don't you wish to examine it more closely?"

"No!" I cried out, the word sharp and desperate. "I recognized him instantly—it's him!"

"Is it the one you saw in the shipwreck?" Degado pressed.

I pushed myself away from him, striving for composure. Once the tempest within me settled, I admitted, "Yes, it's him. I've seen him."

Degado seated himself across from me, intrigue mingling with disbelief. "You mean you've encountered his ghost?"

I paused, a sardonic smile tugging at my lips. "No ghost, sir. I fought with him in the water. He's no specter."

Degado inhaled sharply, "He was born in 1614."

The implications hung heavy in the air. He didn't mention a death year—perhaps out of respect for my conviction. But the unspoken skepticism was clear; three centuries separated Ves Degado's birth from today, defying the bounds of mortality.

I groaned softly, "Regardless of his birth year, I encountered him. He attacked me with a hammer, nearly took my life. He commanded those ships to ram mine, sending it beneath the waves, driving me to the brink of madness!"

Words faltered as I gasped for air, fear and disbelief swirling within me. A dark premonition loomed, whispering of impending madness.

Degado, noticing the turmoil etched on my face, swiftly handed me a glass of wine. I downed it in one swift motion, the warmth spreading through me, momentarily tethering me to sanity.

Degado meticulously returned everything to the box, sealing its secrets away. Once I regained a semblance of composure, he offered a sincere apology, "I'm so sorry."

His reluctance to revisit the topic was palpable, yet he couldn't resist adding, "Our family records describe him as a man of fierce temperament—he even killed a crew member with his own hands."

I remained silent, absorbing the gravity of his words. Degado continued, "I'm truly sorry for stirring such emotions. I had a suggestion, but perhaps it's best left unsaid."

A bitter smile touched my lips. "What was your suggestion? To dive beneath the sea once more?"

Degado shook his head. "No, returning would be futile. You've been there, and nothing was uncovered. Many dismissed your experience as mere hallucination. But was it truly that? Was it?"

I chuckled without humor, "An illusion? How could I conjure a man from my mind whom I recognized instantly, despite never having seen him before?"

"If it wasn't a hallucination—and we must consider it wasn't—then another explanation is needed," Degado reasoned.

"Yes," I replied, my voice weary yet resolute. "We must entertain the notion that this ancient Mr. Degado somehow endures, living freely beneath the waves. He and his ships remain."

I uttered the thought in a single breath, then inhaled deeply before voicing the haunting question, "But is such a thing possible?"

The room fell into a heavy silence, the air thick with the impossible. The notion seemed absurd, yet the evidence of my own senses defied logic. The idea of a man, centuries old, navigating the depths of the ocean with his ghostly fleet, was as thrilling as it was terrifying. And in that silence, the mysteries of the Degado lineage loomed larger than ever, challenging the boundaries of belief and reason.

Degado paced the room, an air of urgency in his step. "If you're interested," he began, "I can share some details. Ves Degado was a man of volatile temperament, shrouded in mystery. There was a time when he secluded himself in the castle, forbidding anyone from approaching or serving him."

I looked at Degado, puzzled by his intent in sharing this information.

"I suspect he was engaged in some clandestine work during that time," Degado speculated. "Though rumors later branded him a traitor plotting rebellion, I don't buy it."

"What do you think he was up to?" I asked.

Degado spread his hands, frustration evident. "I don't know. But my initial thought was to—"

I interrupted, the realization striking me. "Wait, you mentioned that since he vanished at sea, no one has entered the castle, correct?"

Degado blinked, nodding slowly.

"Which means," I continued, "the castle has remained untouched for three centuries?"

He nodded again, a spark of excitement in his eyes.

"I see," I said, piecing it together. "You want to explore the castle. If anything remains, we might uncover what he was working on."

"Exactly!" Degado exclaimed, his enthusiasm palpable. "I intended to invite you to join me."

I stood, then settled back into my seat, contemplating the proposition. "Exploring the castle might reveal his past, but it won't necessarily explain my encounter under the sea."

Degado shook his head. "On the contrary, you saw him in the depths, yet he's nowhere to be found now. How could he appear after three centuries? I believe his past holds clues to this mystery."

I pondered his words, the weight of past traumas pressing on my mind. "Mr. Degado, this ordeal has brought misfortune to many. I narrowly escaped ending up in an asylum. What drives you to pursue this?"

"To uncover the truth about the most extraordinary figure in my family's history," he replied, resolved.

I studied him, sensing his determination. "In a week, if you're not coming, I'll proceed alone," he added. "You have time to decide."

I sighed, rubbing my face wearily. "I'll accompany you, but let's keep it between us."

"Certainly," Degado agreed, "and it will remain confidential."

We sealed our pact with a toast, and then delved into the contents of the box, pouring over the documents late into the night. In the days that followed, we worked closely together, piecing together fragments of Ves Degado's enigmatic life.

As the week progressed, I uncovered several intriguing leads within the castle's history, each hinting at secrets long buried beneath the weight of time.

First, the construction of the three ships was enveloped in a veil of secrecy, meticulously orchestrated by General Ves Degado. As the overseer, Ves Degado enforced an ironclad rule of exclusivity—only those directly involved in the project were permitted near the site. Even the emperor's envoy found himself barred from entry, a bold move that incited a political tempest.

Accusations of insubordination and disrespect toward the emperor swirled, yet somehow, the storm was quelled, leaving Ves Degado's authority intact.

Second, the project was marked by an unusual level of compartmentalization. Each craftsman worked in isolation, forbidden from communicating with their peers about the work they were doing. This strict separation was enforced with ruthless severity—those who dared to breach the rule were executed on the spot.

Third, the cost of constructing the ships was astronomical. By contemporary standards, the resources could have produced thirty vessels of equal size. The emperor's surprising tolerance of this extravagance suggested a tacit understanding with Ves Degado, hinting at a secretive agenda.

Finally, only the exteriors of the ships were known. Their interiors remained a mystery, even at the time of construction. One craftsman, who spoke of the wood's superior quality and its special preservation treatment, vanished soon after.

From these details, it was clear Ves Degado was orchestrating an extraordinary endeavor, and the ships harbored a profound secret. Moreover, it seemed likely that the emperor was complicit, or at least aware of the significance.

The notion that the three ships could still be sailing the seas, appearing as if summoned from the mists of time, seemed beyond belief. Yet, I had witnessed them firsthand. Not only did they appear before me, but they also collided with my vessel, a haunting reality I could not escape.

I had ventured into one of these spectral ships and vividly recalled the interior—preserved and vibrant, as though untouched by centuries beneath the waves. These memories were etched into my mind, unforgettable and undeniable.

With the revelation that General Ves Degado's secretive endeavors were intimately tied to these ships, our resolve to investigate his ancestral castle intensified. The possibility of uncovering answers within its forgotten halls beckoned irresistibly.

Flora was determined to accompany me, her insistence fueled by the fear of another catastrophe like the one that nearly shattered my sanity. I assured her that there would be no danger this time. Our task, I believed, was straightforward: using the keys to unlock the castle's doors and explore its rooms, a task even two young men could manage.

I genuinely believed in the simplicity of our mission, not intending to coax Flora. Yet, as events would unfold, the reality proved far more complex than I had anticipated, stretching beyond the bounds of my imagination.

Degado and I set off for Spain, where his esteemed status opened doors to numerous social engagements. While these initial days were filled with mundane formalities, they served merely as a prelude to our true purpose. On the second night, we embarked on our journey to the castle, driven by the promise of unraveling a mystery that spanned centuries and defied reason.

Little did we know, the secrets we were about to uncover would stretch the limits of our understanding, challenging everything we thought we knew about the past—and the present.

Our journey to the castle was a grueling one, with Degado and I taking turns at the wheel. Nearly forty hours on the road brought us to our destination just as the midday sun bathed the landscape in golden light.

Standing before the castle, the view was breathtaking. The sea crashed against the cliffs below, its relentless rhythm echoing through the air, sending salty spray high into the sky. It was easy to see why old Degado had chosen this dramatic location, his passion for the ocean reflected in the castle's perch above the tumultuous waves.

The castle itself, however, was more dilapidated than I had anticipated. Built from massive stones, it had withstood the test of time with a certain dignity, yet nature had begun to reclaim it. Vines, half-withered and clinging to life, draped over the structure, giving it a forlorn, almost mystical appearance, reminiscent of a wizard's abode from a fairy tale.

As I surveyed the castle, my imagination ran wild, picturing windows thrown open to release a flurry of crows, with a witch trailing on a broomstick.

I shared my whimsical thoughts with Degado, but he didn't share my sense of humor. "I don't think my family has anything to do with witchcraft," he replied, stone-faced.

I chose not to clarify, sensing his pride in his family's legacy. Sometimes, silence was the better part of valor. We lingered by the car, taking in the sight from ten yards before the imposing iron gate. Degado sighed, "It's even older than when I last visited. I considered hiring craftsmen to restore it—"

His words trailed off, and a bitter smile played on his lips. The cost of restoring such a grand edifice would indeed be astronomical, beyond the means of most wealthy individuals.

We approached the iron gate, its massive emblem of the Degado family now obscured by rust. The iron hinges were similarly decayed, flaking at the slightest touch.

Degado inserted a key into the oversized keyhole, only to find it immovable.

With a rueful grin, he and I tugged on the gate until it surrendered, collapsing with a groan of protest. We returned to the car and drove through the gate into a vast courtyard.

The courtyard was a testament to time's passage, strewn with broken stone statues and a dry pool filled with dead leaves. At its center stood a stone sea monster, itself a victim of time's ravages.

We navigated through the overgrown grounds, the tires crunching over grass that had long since obscured the path, making strange, plaintive noises. Finally, we stopped before the castle's entrance, the threshold of our journey into the past—and perhaps, into the heart of the mystery that had compelled us here.

Chapter 10

The Castle

The castle's oak gate stood imposingly, its weathered surface still sturdy despite the years. Stone steps led up to it, overrun with weeds that clung stubbornly to our trousers as we ascended.

As we reached the door, Degado gave it a firm push, only to step back as a cascade of dust descended. Even in broad daylight, the sight sent a shiver down my spine—a reminder of the castle's long abandonment.

Once the dust settled, Degado retrieved a key from his collection, inserting it into the lock. The mechanism, surprisingly free of rust, yielded with a "click."

"Get ready!" he warned, though I wasn't sure what for. Covering his head with one hand, he pushed the door open with the other.

The door creaked open with an eerie wail, releasing a wave of indescribable odor that assaulted our senses. We recoiled instinctively, the stench almost palpable—a miasma of decay, or as I would later think of it, "the smell of death."

Regaining his composure, Degado kicked the door wider, revealing the shadowy grandeur of the lobby within. Above us, the ceiling teemed with thousands of bats. Disturbed by the sudden influx of light, they took flight en masse, their wings stirring clouds of dust that fell like snowflakes.

The sight was both mesmerizing and alarming. "We can't go in—there are too many bats!" I exclaimed.

Degado shook his head, resolute. "Last time, I tried to drive them out, but it was futile. We must proceed regardless."

I hesitated, my mind racing with cautionary tales of rabies and airborne pathogens. "Bats can spread disease. Even the air they inhabit can be dangerous."

Degado nodded, acknowledging the risk. "I know, but I was here before and emerged unscathed."

Faced with no alternative, we improvised. Removing our coats, we wrapped them around our heads, leaving only our eyes exposed. It was a small measure of protection against the swirling chaos of wings.

Once inside, we quickly shut the door, plunging the hall into darkness. Gradually, the bats resettled, and the oppressive fluttering eased.

We moved cautiously to the center of the hall, where six massive pillars loomed. At the heart of them stood an imposing statue—an heroic figure with one foot upon a half-sunken ship, the other hand brandishing a sword.

The statue before us was enigmatic, possibly a tribute to a Degado ancestor or even Ves Degado himself. Yet, its identity was obscured by layers of bat droppings, rendering the face indistinct, its features lost to neglect and time.

Behind the statue were two imposing doors, flanked by grand staircases that spiraled into the shadows above.

The air was thick with the scent of history, tinged with decay.

"We have no map of this place," Degado remarked, his voice echoing softly in the vastness.

"When you came last time—" I began, but he cut me off with a shake of his head. "I only ventured as far as we stand now. The state of things was overwhelming, and I withdrew."

I couldn't fault him for his caution. Anyone encountering this scene would likely retreat without a compelling reason to press on. But our purpose was clear, and retreat was not an option for us now.

I surveyed the space, contemplating our next move. "Typically, the room behind the lobby would be the owner's study. We should start there."

Degado nodded in agreement, and we navigated around the statue to the doors beyond.

Once, a velvet curtain had hung between the statue and the doors, but now, only tattered remnants remained, entombed in dust. I looked at the fragments and couldn't suppress a wry smile. "It seems bats aren't our only concern. I'd wager this place is home to at least ten thousand rats."

Degado remained silent, his expression unreadable as he bent down to retrieve a key from his collection.

The room was shrouded in darkness, with only a few high windows allowing in muted light. The outside vines blocked much of the view, while layers of dust inside reduced visibility to mere silhouettes.

Degado finally located the key and unlocked the door, sliding it open to reveal an interior cloaked in shadow, yet seemingly free of bats. Without flashlights, we relied on instinct, stepping inside and closing the door to avoid disturbing the colony in the lobby.

As we groped through the gloom, my hand brushed against a table. Degado produced a lighter, its small flame casting flickering shadows that danced across the walls.

In this dim light, I noticed heavy curtains. I moved to draw them open, hoping to let in more light, but as soon as I touched them, they collapsed, enveloping me in a suffocating embrace. Instantly, I was plunged into darkness, dust cascading into my nose, mouth, and eyes, leaving me gasping and coughing.

Panicked, I clawed at the fabric, feeling like I was wrestling a sea serpent in the depths. Degado rushed to my aid, and together we ripped the ancient curtains apart. The fabric was so brittle it tore easily, yet the dust persisted, blinding and choking me.

For several minutes, I could do nothing but cough and rub my eyes. Tears streamed down my face, and Degado patted my back, offering what comfort he could. "In a castle sealed for centuries, every corner is a potential trap. We must be cautious," he advised.

His words, though sincere, seemed almost laughable after my ordeal. Despite spitting out dust repeatedly, it felt as though my mouth was still coated in grit, leaving me feeling foolish and embarrassed.

With a weary smile, I nodded. "Let's just get to work."

The fallen curtains allowed some light to filter in through the windows, enough to discern the outlines of objects in the room.

The study room was a testament to Ves Degado's obsession with ships. Shelves lined the walls, but instead of books, they held an array of ship models. These models, each about two meters long, were once intricate replicas of majestic vessels. Now, time had reduced them to fragile silhouettes, their former glory obscured by layers of dust and decay.

There were at least seventy or eighty models, surrounding a grand desk at the room's center. The desk, too, was buried under a thick blanket of dust. I gestured to Degado, "Let's see what's on the table."

Degado, absorbed in examining a model, joined me at the desk.

The dust on the table was so thick, it had formed a sponge-like layer that could be peeled off in one piece. As I brushed away the dust with my hand, a goose feather emerged from underneath, resting atop a piece of parchment. The paper bore a single line of text, its ink preserved through the years: "I am the greatest person in the world!"

Below the boastful claim was a signature.

Degado's eyes widened in recognition. "That's his signature. I've seen it before."

It was clear that "he" referred to Ves Degado. I mused aloud, "Quite the declaration. He certainly thought highly of himself."

Degado's smile was tinged with irony. "Arrogance was a hallmark of his character."

I lifted the parchment, marveling at its resilience. Despite centuries, it remained intact. "It's as if he wanted to ensure his greatness was known."

I paused, contemplating the implications. "If he's truly survived beneath the sea all this time, perhaps he is the greatest man."

Degado dusted off more of the desk, uncovering sailors' rulers and a slim book. The book, however, was so brittle it began to disintegrate as I handled it. Carefully, I held the fragments, revealing its contents. Surprisingly, it was a book on marine life from Ves Degado's era.

We rifled through the desk's drawers but found little of note—just some gold coins and trivial items.

Degado sighed, disheartened. "It seems his study yields no secrets."

I frowned, unwilling to concede. "If he concealed anything about the ships' construction, it would surely be here in his study."

Degado straightened, his gaze sweeping the room. As our eyes adjusted to the dim light, he seemed drawn to the ship models.

I picked up one of the models, only for its brittle hull to crumble in my hands. It was a stark reminder of the passage of time, and yet, I couldn't shake the feeling that these models held clues to the mystery we sought to unravel.

Upon accidentally breaking the hull of one of the ship models, I discovered the intricacy with which they were crafted. The details were astounding—not just the exterior, but the inner compartments and furnishings were meticulously represented. "Digado, you have to see how finely these models are made!" I exclaimed.

Digado joined me, peering closely. "If only we could find models of the three ships," he mused. His meaning was clear: while we knew the ships' exteriors, their interiors remained a mystery. Even from my brief time aboard one, the cabins had offered no clear insight.

If these models included those of the three ships, we might finally uncover their secrets. With renewed determination, we examined each ship, but our search ended in disappointment. After hours of scrutiny, we conceded that the study held no answers.

We left the study, the stairs groaning ominously beneath our feet as we ascended. The upper floor was a warren of rooms, each devoured half an hour at a time. By the sixth room, night had fallen, and the castle was swallowed by darkness.

With no discoveries to show for our efforts, the castle took on a more sinister air. The bats below emitted eerie sounds that echoed through the corridors.

"We should leave for now," I suggested. "We need proper tools to continue our search tomorrow."

At first, Digado seemed lost in thought, ignoring my words. When I repeated myself, he replied, "You go ahead. I'm staying."

I was taken aback. "What do you mean, staying? You can't spend the night here. There's nowhere to sleep!"

"I'm fine in the study," Digado insisted. "The wooden chairs are serviceable."

"Why not just come back tomorrow?" I pressed.

"You don't understand," he said, his voice resolute. "This castle is part of my heritage. I feel connected to it in a way you can't. It's not just a structure—it's my family's legacy."

He paused, then added, "Go on without me. I'll be here when you return."

Despite my repeated attempts to change his mind, Digado remained firm. Resigned, I descended the stairs with him.

As I wrapped my coat around my head and dashed out of the hall, I glanced back to see him standing behind the statue. In the dim light, he seemed as much a part of the castle as the stone figures themselves.

An hour after leaving Digado at the castle, I found myself in a small-town bar, nursing a beer. The patrons, familiar faces to one another, eyed me, the outsider, with curiosity. Before long, a young man approached, a friendly smile on his face. "Not often we see strangers here.

Your car's quite the sight—we've never seen one like it before!"

As he spoke, the bar fell silent, all ears on our conversation. I returned his smile. "The car isn't mine; it belongs to my friend, Mr. Degado."

At the mention of Degado's name, the young man's demeanor shifted. He trembled slightly, spilling some of his drink, and the others mirrored his shock.

"Why? What's the matter?" I asked, genuinely puzzled.

The young man forced a weak smile. "Nothing, really. It's just that your friend's name is connected to an old castle nearby—Degado Castle."

I nodded, acknowledging the connection. "Yes, I spent the afternoon there. It belongs to Mr. Degado."

His reaction was immediate and visceral. He staggered back, knocking over a chair, while an older man hurried to steady him, a protective gesture. The eyes of everyone in the bar were fixed on me, filled with an unsettling mix of disbelief and fear.

I rose to my feet, and the young man, now steadied, shouted, "You're lying! No one goes to that castle—it's haunted! Anyone who does is doomed!"

I chuckled softly, resuming my seat. "You're mistaken. I've been there, and I'm still here. Mr. Degado stayed the night, and I'm sure he'll be fine as well."

Silence washed over the bar, save for an old woman clasping her hands in prayer. Their reactions didn't surprise me; every ancient building harbors ghost stories, and the locals' firm belief in such tales was likely all that kept the castle intact, untouched for centuries.

Not wishing to disrupt their evening, I settled my bill and returned to my hotel, where I slept soundly. The next morning, I busied myself in town, gathering supplies for our continued exploration.

Around noon, I arrived back at the castle, calling out cheerfully, "Degado, look what I've brought for you!"

Arms laden with provisions, I called again, but received no response. Concerned, I donned my makeshift headgear, a bamboo basket, and armed with a flashlight, ventured inside. The basket provided some protection from the bats as I made my way to the study.

Opening the door, I found Degado slumped in a chair, head lolling as if asleep. I approached, shaking him gently. "You must be starving!"

Slowly, he lifted his head, revealing a face unnaturally pale. Alarmed, I remarked, "You look awful. I told you not to spend the night here!"

His lips trembled as he whispered, "Do you have any wine?"

Seeing he was in no fit state, I helped him to his feet, covering his head with the basket, and guided him out to the sunlit lawn. The moment I released him, he collapsed, the basket rolling away. On all fours, he gasped for air.

I hurried to the car, returning with a thermos of hot coffee. His hands shook as he drank, but the warmth revived him, bringing a hint of color back to his cheeks. He managed to stand, albeit shakily.

"What happened last night?" I pressed, worried about his state.

Digado drew a deep breath, shaking his head. "Nothing. I just stayed in the study."

I scrutinized Digado, his face still bearing traces of the night's ordeal. "You look quite frightening," I remarked with concern.

He offered a rueful smile. "Honestly, after midnight, my imagination got the better of me. I fell into a state of sheer terror, almost like a semi-coma. It's hard to avoid when you're alone in a place like this."

I didn't intend to mock him, but I couldn't resist pointing out, "This is your castle. You have a connection to it. Why did it affect you so?"

His smile was tinged with irony. "You have no idea how many bizarre noises come from this place in the dead of night."

I gave him a reassuring pat on the shoulder. "But you didn't actually see anything, did you?"

His expression slowly relaxed. "I wish I had seen something concrete, but no. It was all just my mind playing tricks, fueled by fear."

Gazing at the vine-covered castle basked in sunlight, I asked, "So, do you still have the courage to continue our search?"

"Absolutely," he replied without hesitation. "As long as you're with me, I won't be afraid."

I nodded in agreement. We laid out a mat on the grass and enjoyed the food I had brought, washing it down with nearly a bottle of wine. Feeling fortified, we re-entered the castle.

Armed with tools, our exploration was more efficient this time. We forced open the windows in each room, though many gave way entirely with their frames, victims of time's relentless march. Yet, despite our thorough search, the hours ticked by fruitlessly.

Eventually, our focus shifted to the cellar. It was expansive, filled with wine and various items, but none held the answers we sought.

As dusk began to settle, casting long shadows across the grounds, I suggested, "Let's call it a day and return tomorrow."

To my surprise, Digado, seemingly recovered from the morning's ordeal, insisted, "You go ahead. I'll remain here."

His stubbornness evoked a mix of amusement and exasperation. "Digado, I found you half-dead this morning. I don't want to come back to find a corpse tomorrow."

He shook his head with determination. "No, I'm staying."

Degado's obstinance and irrational determination to stay in the castle infuriated me. "Staying here will drive you mad!" I shouted, my voice echoing in the vastness of the castle.

He shot back defiantly, "I'll do what I want. You have no right to tell me otherwise!"

His sudden hostility baffled me. After his harrowing night, it made no sense for him to insist on staying.

It wasn't until much later, after discussing the situation with friends, that I gained some insight. A psychologist suggested that Degado's behavior was a result of the castle's oppressive atmosphere combined with his deep-seated familial pride. The castle, a symbol of his heritage, evoked a profound emotional response, compelling him to stay despite his fear. Whether this analysis was accurate, I couldn't say. In the moment, I didn't have the luxury of pondering psychological motivations. I simply resolved to remove him from the situation. "You don't need to shout," I retorted. "I'm taking you out of here tonight."

With that, I grabbed his arm, determined to lead him out. Despite his protests and resistance, I was stronger, and he had little choice but to follow as I pulled him from the cellar. His frustration boiled over, manifesting in a kick at the debris scattered around us.

Ignoring his outburst, I dragged him through the passage, into the main hall, and finally released him by the statue, expecting him to follow me out.

What happened next was completely unforeseen. As soon as I let go, Degado, in a fit of rage, swung a punch at me.

The blow, unexpected and forceful, caught me on the chin, sending a sharp pain through my jaw. I stumbled backward, anger and surprise mingling in my cry. My momentum carried me back into the statue, which, to my shock, toppled under the impact.

The chain reaction set off by the statue's fall was catastrophic, far beyond anything I could have imagined. What started as a simple struggle ended in chaos as the ancient structure gave way under the strain.

The statue, once a stoic guardian of the hall, crashed to the floor, its impact reverberating through the castle. In an instant, it was as if the entire building had decided to collapse in protest. The middle section of the stairs crumbled, sending debris cascading down. Above us, the ceiling gave way, releasing clouds of dust and sending thousands of bats into a frenzied flight.

The cacophony of destruction was overwhelming: the crash of stone, the screech of disturbed bats, the relentless din of debris hitting the floor. It sounded as if the entire castle was on the verge of becoming a ruin.

Amidst the chaos, Degado's voice reached out, calling my name. But the noise and dust made it impossible to discern his words clearly. I could only make out the desperation in his voice as I instinctively covered my head and crouched low, eyes squeezed shut against the onslaught of dust and debris.

The statue's collapse triggered a chain reaction that took ten minutes to cease. When the noise finally stopped and I opened my eyes, I discovered that a large section of the wall at the gate had also crumbled.

Chapter 11

Bones Beneath the Passage

The ten minutes of chaos felt interminable, but once the dust settled and the noise ceased, the scene transformed.

The bats had fled, leaving the castle in eerie silence, and the setting sun cast its golden light through the breaches in the walls. Outside, the bats' flight against the backdrop of the sunset was a strange, mesmerizing sight.

Despite the unexpected beauty of the moment, my focus remained on finding Degado. I spotted him on the ground, shakily getting to his feet, muttering in a daze, "Oh my god, Ash, I didn't mean to hurt you. I really didn't mean to hurt you!"

Relieved that he was unharmed, I approached, calling out, "Stop talking to God—you didn't hurt me!"

His eyes found mine, relief washing over his face. He grasped my hand tightly, his earlier panic replaced by gratitude.

I gave his shoulder a reassuring pat, suggesting we head back to town, but Degado suddenly pointed behind me, exclaiming, "Look!"

Turning, I was taken aback by what I saw.

The towering statue had stood on a stone base. When it fell, it shattered into countless pieces, but the stone base was only partially removed. Degado and I could clearly see that the center of the base was hollow, and inside the hollow part, there was a capstan with an iron cable coiled around it.

Those iron cables, mysteriously coated with oil, had never rusted!

Degado, equally astounded, gestured in disbelief. "What is this?"

Excitement surged through me. "Don't you see? There's another secret room in this castle. The capstan controls the mechanism to open it. Let's do it!"

We grabbed the handle and heaved it downward. Initially resistant, the capstan required our combined strength to turn. But as it completed one rotation, the effort eased. On the second turn, a distinct "click" echoed from the hall's center.

We spun around, watching as a square section of the floor rose steadily. Our hearts raced with anticipation. As soon as the floor was fully upright, revealing an opening, we trained our flashlights on it.

A stone staircase spiraled downward, its depths obscured by darkness. Intrigued, Degado declared, "Don't even think about suggesting we come back tomorrow. I want to explore now!"

I chuckled. "No one said anything about waiting until tomorrow!"

With that, Degado descended, the narrow steps allowing only single-file passage. I followed closely, both of us armed with flashlights.

The staircase, clearly man-made, ended after about thirty steps, giving way to a natural stone crevice.

Degado's flashlight beam sliced through the darkness, revealing a ladder of iron rings embedded in the stone wall, stretching down into the abyss. He glanced up, his face a mask of uncertainty. "There are iron rings going all the way down."

"Test them to see if they're secure," I urged, my voice echoing slightly in the confined space.

With a cautious nod, Degado reached out, placing his foot into one of the rings. I held his hand, feeling the tension in his muscles as he shifted his weight. A metallic "click" resonated through the cavern, but the ring held firm.

"They're solid!" he exclaimed, relief evident in his voice.

I released his hand, watching as he began his descent. It was as if the darkness itself was slowly consuming him, the shadows swallowing him whole. His face reappeared briefly, peering up at me. "Maybe you should wait up there until I check it out."

I shook my head, dismissing the idea immediately. "No way. We venture together. Hold on, I'm coming."

His body gradually disappeared into the unknown. Carefully, I followed. I found the first iron ring with my right foot, gripping the stone ledge with my hands as I groped downward with my left. Each ring was spaced about a foot apart, making our descent manageable.

These rings were clearly man-made, but the passage itself was a natural formation, carved by ancient forces within the mountain's belly. Perhaps the castle builders had stumbled upon this secret by chance, or maybe the fortress was deliberately constructed atop this hidden labyrinth, its entrance concealed until now. The truth was lost to time.

As Degado led the way, I followed closely, the tunnel shifting from expansive to claustrophobically narrow, forcing us to squeeze through. It occurred to me that anyone larger might find themselves wedged immovably between the mountain's stony jaws.

Descending, I counted the rings, our flashlights clamped between our teeth, casting eerie shadows. The air was thick, oppressive, making each breath a labor.

"How far down do you think we are?" I called, my voice reverberating in the tight space.

Degado's voice floated back, tinged with awe. "It feels like we're diving to the earth's core!"

I chuckled, though my mind raced with possibilities. "No, this cliff is about three hundred feet high. It could lead to the sea."

His excitement was palpable. "Yes, the sea! I can smell the salt in the air!"

His words seemed fanciful, but as we descended further, the unmistakable scent of the ocean reached me. The air grew damper, the iron rings slick with rust, challenging our grip. Finally, the beam of our flashlights caught the glimmer of water below. We landed on a massive stone slab, relief washing over us.

In that moment, the cave revealed its secrets. It was vast, its walls echoing with the sound of our breaths and the distant murmur of the sea. Before us, the sea lapped gently at large, flat stones, clearly shaped by human hands. Bridges once linked these stones, but time or calamity had broken them, leaving no apparent escape from this hidden enclave.

The cave was an enigma sealed within stone, its only known entrance the secret passage we had uncovered. The sea lapped at our feet, a dark and mysterious expanse whispering of unknown dangers lurking beneath its surface. Though I believed that diving might lead to an exit, the risks were uncharted and potentially perilous.

Our flashlights cut through the gloom, revealing a massive iron box perched atop a large stone. Its sheer size rendered it immovable, suggesting that it had been constructed in situ, piece by piece. The box towered three meters high, stretched over five meters long, and spanned nearly four meters wide, its surface cloaked in the heavy rust of ages.

Beside the colossal box, two smaller iron structures rested, their dimensions and shapes uncannily reminiscent of coffins. As soon as my eyes fell upon these three iron monoliths, my heartbeat quickened with anticipation. I turned to Degado, and the shared excitement in his eyes mirrored my own. It was clear we both sensed the same truth: our journey was reaching its climax, and the answers we sought lay within these enigmatic containers.

Our reasoning felt sound. The cave, accessible only through a clandestine passageway, surely harbored secrets of great significance. Why else would such measures be taken to conceal its contents, unless they were of extraordinary importance? The presence of the iron boxes, hidden away in this secluded cavern, whispered of mysteries long buried and now beckoning to be uncovered.

Without warning, Degado lunged forward, ready to dive into the water. Instinctively, I grabbed his arm. "What are you doing?" I demanded.

His voice echoed through the cavern, charged with urgency. "I'm going to swim over and see what's inside those boxes!"

I aimed my flashlight at the water, its depths appearing black and foreboding. While I admired Degado's bravery, his rashness infuriated me. "How can you be certain the water's safe? We should return with better lighting before diving in headfirst!"

He hesitated, but swiftly dismissed my caution. "It's only twenty feet to the rock. We can make it!"

As I scooped a handful of seawater, its clarity was apparent despite the deceptive darkness created by our limited lighting. The water's calm surface belied the potential for unseen currents beneath. To test this, I rolled up pieces of paper and tossed them into the water. Degado, impatient, watched my cautious experiment with skepticism.

"In caves like this," I explained, "hidden vortices can be treacherous. They might drag you under without warning."

As we observed, the paper rolls drifted slowly in a uniform direction, revealing a gentle undercurrent. However, its pace was too sluggish to pose any real threat. Before I could articulate my thoughts, Degado, emboldened by the apparent safety, decided to act.

"See? No danger!" he proclaimed, plunging into the water with a splash. His body disappeared momentarily, then resurfaced as he swam confidently toward the large rock.

In less than a minute, he stood triumphant on the rock's surface. Inspired by his success, I followed, holding my flashlight aloft as I entered the cold, bracing water. The swim was brief, and soon I too clambered onto the rock beside him. We wrung out our clothes, laying them to dry under the dim cave light.

Our attention turned to the three iron boxes. Each was sealed with a lock, the smaller two boasting external mechanisms. With a determined twist, I snapped the lock from one, the metal yielding easily to my efforts.

Degado followed my lead, deftly twisting the lock on the remaining small iron box. As we each lifted the lids, the metal creaked, and the rusty hinges protested. The lids rose just enough to eclipse our view, hiding the contents within.

Our actions mirrored one another's. I peered inside, and my hand involuntarily released the lid, allowing it to crash shut with a resounding "bang," a cloud of rust cascading to the ground.

We exchanged glances, our faces painted with expressions of disbelief and a hint of dread. I could feel the involuntary twitch of my facial muscles, mirroring the shock and bewilderment I read on Degado's face.

After a tense silence, I broke the stalemate. "What did you find in yours?"

He met my question with one of his own. "What's in yours?"

"A skeleton," I admitted, the word hanging heavily in the air.

Degado's grim smile said it all as he gestured to his own iron box. "Same here."

The realization hit us both with the force of an unexpected blow. From the moment we'd laid eyes on the iron boxes, their coffin-like dimensions had been apparent, but the reality was far more jarring than any speculation.

The shock of uncovering the skeletal remains had been enough to make me drop the lid. I imagined Degado had experienced the same visceral reaction. However, with the initial surprise behind us, we resolved to examine the contents more thoroughly.

We reopened the lids, this time more deliberately. I applied pressure to keep mine open, and with a satisfying "snap," the rusty chain securing the lid gave way. The lid clattered onto the stone, sending ripples across the water as it slid into the depths.

Peering into the box, I confirmed my suspicions. The iron box had indeed served as a makeshift coffin. Beneath the skeletal remains, I discerned the remnants of what might once have been silk, now decayed beyond recognition.

The skeleton was remarkably long, and certain anomalies quickly became apparent. This was no ordinary set of bones—there was only one leg, elongated and devoid of toes, suggesting the remains of a disabled individual.

As I studied the macabre sight, Degado's voice rang out with a revelation. "It's the skeleton of a one-legged man!"

I was momentarily stunned, processing the strange reality before us. Degado's words about the "one-legged man" echoed in my mind. The realization struck me as I examined the bones in my own iron box: another "one-legged man."

I joined Degado at his side, peering into the box before him. Indeed, the skeleton mirrored the one in my box.

The identical nature of these remains was unsettling. I leaned closer, allowing the beam of my flashlight to glide over the skeletal frame.

An acrid stench wafted up from the open box, compelling me to cover my nose. There was no mistaking the human origin of the remains: the skull bore seven distinct holes, the teeth were sharp and pointed, and the sternum and spine were robust. The arms were unusually long, with particularly elongated finger bones.

Yet below the waist, the structure defied human anatomy. The pelvis was narrow, and the leg bones extended in six or seven segments, unlike any human leg which typically comprised three sections with a foot. These skeletons ended in a peculiar, flat bone, devoid of any toes.

It dawned on me what Degado had meant by "one-legged man." He hadn't been referring to someone who had lost a leg, but to someone born with only one leg. The absence of any secondary leg, coupled with the strange leg structure, confirmed this.

Rising, I turned to Degado. "What kind of person do you think these remains belonged to? What would they have looked like in life?"

Degado's face was a mask of uncertainty. "This person was tall, taller than either of us, and had only one leg..." He gestured, trying to visualize. "With just one leg, they'd have to hop to move. Look at those leg bones—I think they must have been able to jump quite high—"

I interrupted, shaking my head. "I disagree. Look at the foot bones—there are no toes, and such flat feet wouldn't allow for high jumps. Any creature capable of jumping relies on foot muscles to propel itself."

Degado's gaze traveled from the bones to me, his breath quickening. His lips moved, but no sound emerged. He seemed on the brink of a revelation, something so bizarre that it left him visibly shaken.

"What is it?" I pressed.

Pointing at the bones, Degado tapped his head, his expression one of disbelief. "It must be my imagination," he finally whispered.

I pressed Degado for clarity. "What exactly are you thinking?"

He hesitated, then said, "I think we've misunderstood. This person didn't have legs at all!"

His words left me momentarily speechless. No legs? Yet, the long bone we saw—how could that be explained? But then, as if a veil lifted from my mind, understanding dawned on me.

Unlike Degado, who had been struck silent by his realization, I shouted in excitement, "Yes, it's not a leg—it's a tail!"

Degado's eyes met mine, wide with amazement. "So, what does this mean? A person with a long tail?"

My voice trembled with revelation, yet I managed to articulate the thought. "Degado, it's not just any tail—it's a fish tail. This skeleton belonged to a creature with a human upper body and a fish lower body. It's a mermaid! A mermaid from the depths of the sea!"

Degado's hands fluttered in the air, a mix of exhilaration and disbelief. "A mermaid, yes, it's a mermaid!"

Overwhelmed, I sank down beside the iron box. The word "mermaid" conjured images from myths and sailors' tales—those half-human, half-fish beings that had tantalized human imagination for centuries. Sailors claimed sightings, only for scientists to dismiss them as misidentified dugongs, creatures bearing little resemblance to the enchanting mermaids of lore.

Yet here, before us, lay bones that defied scientific skepticism. Could these really be the remains of mermaids? The notion seemed fantastical, yet inexplicably plausible given the evidence.

The vastness of the ocean, with its myriad mysteries, had always eluded full human understanding. While mermaids were relegated to the realm of fiction, who could truly claim to know all the secrets the sea harbored?

I sat in silence, grappling with the enormity of our discovery. Degado stood nearby, equally lost in thought. Neither of us spoke, each absorbed in the gravity of what we had uncovered.

Eventually, I rose, my flashlight beam catching on something unexpected. In my haste, I nearly dropped the light into the water but managed to catch it, my movement dislodging more rust from the iron box. As I steadied the flashlight, I noticed something inscribed on the box's side.

"Look here," I called out urgently. "There are words engraved on the box!"

The words promised another layer to the mystery, a potential clue to unraveling the history and purpose of these enigmatic remains.

Degado crouched down beside me, both of us intent on deciphering the words beneath the rust. Slowly, painstakingly, we cleared away the corrosion with our hands, revealing several lines of text etched into the metal. Though time had blurred them, careful scrutiny allowed us to uncover their meaning.

It took us about half an hour, but the effort was rewarded. We exchanged glances, our suspicions confirmed: these were indeed mermaid skeletons. The inscriptions on the iron box read:

"Pétain's body, he was my good friend. No one knew he existed, but he did exist. I believe he was one of the only two mermaids left in the world. He was truly a human, although half of his body was a fish. May he rest in peace!"

With renewed urgency, I moved to the second iron box, wiping away the rust to uncover a similar message. This one bore a different name: "Beth," suggesting that she might have been a female mermaid.

Degado stood, processing the implications. "We set out to uncover the secret of the three ships, and instead, we've found the remains of two mermaids."

I took a deep breath, the gravity of our discovery sinking in. "This is an extraordinary find, Degado. It ties directly to the heart of our quest. Remember, there's that old tale—Ves Degado, a man who lived among the sea folk."

Degado frowned, skeptical. "That's quite a leap. You can't just assume he lived among mermaids."

"Perhaps," I conceded, "but these mermaids lived in the sea, and there's a connection here we can't ignore."

Degado's voice rose, a mix of excitement and incredulity. "But you never claimed to have met a mermaid!"

I shook my head, understanding his agitation. "I didn't say your ancestor was a mermaid, but we can't deny that someone—perhaps Degado—was close to these creatures."

He nodded, and I continued, "We don't know the circumstances of how he encountered the mermaids, but it's likely he shared a part of his life with them."

Despite his skepticism, Degado's curiosity was undeniable. "So what if he did?"

"Think about it," I suggested. "He might have learned from them how to survive in the sea."

Degado's eyes widened, then narrowed as he considered the possibility. His chest heaved with the weight of new thoughts. "Are you saying he's been living in the sea all this time?"

I shrugged. "That's your interpretation. I only mentioned seeing him near a shipwreck on the ocean floor."

Degado's voice sharpened. "Is there a difference?"

I chuckled. "Not really. You're the one drawing the distinction."

He stood in silence, grappling with the implications. "Could he really have such abilities? To live underwater for so long?"

The air around us felt cooler, prompting me to retrieve my still-damp clothes from the stone and slip them on. It was only then that I remembered the massive iron box we had yet to explore.

The enormity of the box, looming beside us, had been overshadowed by the shock of discovering the mermaid skeletons. Now, its mystery beckoned, reigniting our sense of purpose. Whatever lay inside promised to deepen the secrets we had uncovered, and we approached it with renewed determination, eager to unveil the next chapter of this astonishing discovery.

Chapter 12

Mermaid

At this point, I gave the big iron box a frustrated kick. "Enough guessing. Let's find out what's inside!" I declared.

The big box was imposing, towering above us, so Degado and I clambered onto the smaller boxes to gain leverage. But despite our combined efforts, the lid remained stubbornly in place. It was locked—a keyhole taunting us with its necessity—and we needed a key, which we didn't have.

Undeterred, Degado and I jumped down, grabbing stones from the cavern floor. We climbed back up, wielding the stones like makeshift hammers, and began battering the area around the keyhole. Sweat trickled down our faces as we hoped the lock, aged and rusted, would yield to our assault.

Finally, our persistence paid off. The area around the keyhole gave way, and together we heaved against the heavy lid. It budged slightly, and we wedged a stone in the gap to hold it open, but couldn't lift it further.

Standing on tiptoe, we peered inside, flashlight beams piercing the dim interior. The space within was vast enough to resemble a small room. As the light danced over the contents, we saw a collection of odd and rusted items—iron rings, a bed, objects that looked like knives.

Degado and I exchanged puzzled glances. "What is all this?" he asked. "Why lock it away so carefully?"

I shook my head, sharing his confusion. The flashlight beam fell upon a sizable pottery basin in a corner, its contents obscured in shadow. We focused the light, revealing a blackened mass inside, reminiscent of decayed animal organs. The sight was revolting.

"We need to get inside and investigate," I suggested.

Degado hesitated, but we both knew there was no turning back. As we scanned the interior, the flashlight caught a small iron box within the larger one, also locked. Encouraged, we renewed our efforts, finally managing to lift the lid of the big iron box higher by a foot, pushing it forward with all our strength. The lid crashed down with a reverberating clang, striking the two smaller boxes.

The impact was massive, causing the smaller boxes—and our precious mermaid skeletons—to tumble into the water with a series of splashes.

Degado and I cried out in unison, horror-struck.

We knew the incredible scientific value these skeletons held. They were proof of mermaids' existence, evidence that could revolutionize our understanding of marine life and human history by suggesting the possibility of prolonged life beneath the sea.

Yet now, they were lost to the depths. The realization hit us hard, an opportunity of immense significance slipping away with the currents. We stood at the edge of the iron box, stunned, aware of the gravity of what had just happened and the vast implications for what might have been.

We lingered atop the massive iron box, enveloped in a cloud of frustration and disappointment. After a while, Degado seemed to be trying to reassure both of us. "It's okay," he said. "We can dive and retrieve the remains one by one."

I nodded in agreement, and together we climbed over the edge of the large iron box, dropping down into its depths. As I kicked through the rusty tools scattered at the bottom, I realized they resembled surgical instruments. "These look like surgeon's tools," I remarked.

Degado moved toward a small iron box, grabbing it and smashing it against the floor of the larger box. With a loud "bang," the small box burst open, spilling a stack of papers.

Degado picked up the papers, shining his flashlight over them. I watched as his face went pale after reading only a few lines. Clutching the papers tightly, he switched off the flashlight, leaving me in the dark about their contents. "What's written on them?" I pressed.

It took several prompts before Degado finally responded, his voice evasive. "Nothing important," he insisted, "just irrelevant stuff."

His obvious lie infuriated me. We had worked together, uncovering an incredible discovery, yet here he was, withholding crucial information. Worse still, his deception was poorly executed.

My anger flared. "Degado, let's look at those papers together," I demanded. "What do they say?"

He stepped back, glaring at me with a fierce intensity, and hid the papers behind his back. I noticed several sheets tearing in his grip. "Be careful," I warned. "You'll ruin them!"

Degado's breath came in ragged gasps. "Enough," he snapped. "Our exploration ends here. Leave this place—it's mine!"

The audacity of his words left me no choice. I shone my flashlight directly at his face, forcing him to squint against the light, and moved toward him.

But Degado's reaction caught me off guard. As I advanced, he charged at me, knocking the flashlight from my hand and plunging us into darkness. In the pitch blackness, he attacked with a frenzied desperation. It was the first time I had ever fought someone inside an iron box.

Despite his mad aggression, I managed to fend him off and bent down to search for the flashlight. Amidst the chaos, I heard his labored breathing, his footsteps, and his collisions with the iron walls. Finally, I found the flashlight, flicked it on, and saw Degado climbing out of the iron box.

I directed the beam at him and shouted, "Degado!"

He turned, the light illuminating his face, revealing a mix of fear and a desperate need to escape. Then, he twisted his body outward, and I heard his scream followed by the sickening thud of his body hitting the rock below.

I called out to Degado again, but there was no response. Climbing out of the iron box, I hurried to his side. He lay still next to the large box, unconscious but fortunately alive. I shook him, trying to rouse him, but he remained unresponsive.

Faced with a dilemma, I realized I couldn't carry him out of the cave. The passageway was narrow and treacherous, challenging even for someone unharmed. Given Degado's condition, it was impossible for me to transport him alone.

His injuries appeared severe, demanding immediate medical attention. I knew time was against us; every passing moment could be critical. Determined to get help, I left Degado's side, knowing that I had to act quickly to save his life.

I plunged into the water, swimming to the passage entrance. Grasping the iron rings, I began the arduous climb upward. The ascent was grueling, my breath coming in ragged gasps, and the sharp rocks left painful scratches on my skin. Finally, I reached the exit, emerging into the darkness of the hall above. With no time to waste, I avoided using my flashlight and stumbled out of the hall.

Outside, the night was serene, the moon casting a gentle glow. It felt as if I had stepped into another world. I sprinted to my car, started the engine, and sped toward the town. It was midnight when I arrived, the streets silent as the townspeople slept.

I remembered a pharmacy run by the town's sole doctor and headed straight there. Leaping from the car, I pounded on the door, my urgent knocking echoing through the quiet street. My calls eventually roused not only the doctor but also several other curious onlookers.

The doctor appeared, bleary-eyed and in his nightclothes. "Mr. Degado has fallen and needs your help," I explained breathlessly. "Please come with me."

The old doctor frowned as he listened to my urgent plea. "He is in a cave under a tunnel of the castle, Degado Castle. In that cave, we found—" I started to say but halted, realizing the complexity of our discovery couldn't be explained quickly. More importantly, Degado's condition was critical, and time was of the essence.

"He's unconscious," I said urgently. "Please, grab your medical supplies and come with me immediately."

As soon as the words left my mouth, an eerie silence descended upon the crowd that had gathered. The bustling noise had evaporated, replaced by a palpable tension. I glanced around and noticed the fear etched on their faces. Some people at the edges of the group were quietly retreating, while others closer to me feigned indifference, yawning and slowly backing away.

The realization hit me—they were terrified of Degado Castle. The locals held deep-rooted beliefs about the castle being cursed or haunted, a place of evil that they avoided at all costs. Their sudden withdrawal was a testament to their fear of any association with the place.

I didn't need the townspeople—I only needed the doctor. But when I turned back to him, I was shocked to see him retreating into his house.

Desperation surged through me, and I grabbed his arm. "Doctor, you must come with me to save him!"

He turned, meeting my gaze with a conflicted look. His silence stretched on, so I pressed further. "You're a doctor. Someone is injured and needs your help!"

I expected no doctor would deny such a request, but the doctor shook his head. "Young man, I've heard about you two. Did you mention Degado Castle?"

"Yes," I replied quickly. "There's a secret passage leading to a cave inside the mountain. My companion, Mr. Degado, had an accident there."

His expression turned wary, and he shook his head. "Go back to the hotel, sleep until dawn, or leave now."

His refusal was a blow, but it was clear his fear of the castle overpowered his sense of duty. I had to think quickly. Perhaps I could convince him, or find someone else willing to help. Degado's life depended on it, and I couldn't afford to waste any more time.

Left alone in the street with the doctor, frustration boiled inside me. I struggled to keep my composure, my voice sharp with urgency. "Doctor, what are you so afraid of?"

The doctor lifted his hands defensively. "It's not fear, exactly. It's tradition. For hundreds of years, no one from our town has approached Degado Castle. It's been a rule passed down through generations."

"Why?" I demanded.

He sighed, a heavy weight in his voice. "You wouldn't understand, being an outsider. This town has always been insular, our ancestors were renowned shipbuilders. But one night, they were all massacred by General Ves Degado, the castle's owner at the time."

A chill ran down my spine at his words.

"Only one survived long enough to return and warn us," the doctor continued. "He spoke of something unspeakably horrific at the castle, urging us to stay away forever. After relaying the warning, he died. We erected a stone tablet with his words by his grave, a constant reminder. For generations, we've honored that warning."

I shook my head, frustration mingling with disbelief. "But that was centuries ago. I've visited the castle multiple times—it's just an abandoned relic. Right now, there's someone there who desperately needs your help!"

The doctor's eyes hardened. "Especially if it's a descendant of Ves Degado, I won't go."

Seeing no way to sway him, I changed tactics. "At least give me some first aid supplies to help him myself."

He hesitated only briefly before nodding.

Fifteen minutes later, I sped down the deserted road back to the castle, a medical kit beside me. My mind raced with questions. From the doctor, I'd learned of Ves Degado's ruthless actions, killing the shipwrights to protect a secret. But what could be so important that he'd commit such atrocities to keep it hidden?

The mystery of the three ships loomed large. What secrets did they hold that were worth such a high cost?

The thought of Ves Degado's cruelty was haunting. His brutal actions—killing the shipbuilders, crushing my ship, and attacking me without provocation—were chilling to recall. The idea of such a person possibly still alive and lurking beneath the sea was terrifying.

Despite the winding, uneven road, the absence of other vehicles allowed me to drive at full speed, urgency propelling me forward. My mind raced as I pushed the car to its limits, knowing I had to reach the castle as quickly as possible.

As I drove, I kept my eyes on the distance. When I realized I was only three or four kilometers from the castle atop the mountain, an unsettling feeling took hold. Something was happening up there—something significant.

As I drove, a sudden swarm of bats filled the night sky, their screeching cries piercing the air. They dove in chaotic formations, their bodies striking my windshield with unsettling frequency, each impact resonating with a sharp "pat." It was as if nature itself was reacting to some unseen disturbance.

Then, a deep rumbling began to emanate from the direction of the castle. The sound was foreboding, growing in intensity as I neared the top of the mountain. My car bounced over the uneven terrain, urgency driving me forward. But just as the castle came into view, I witnessed a scene that left me breathless.

The last standing wall of the castle trembled, as if it were constructed of sand, and then slowly crumbled, collapsing with a thunderous crash. Dust billowed into the air, creating a dense, swirling cloud that obscured everything in its path.

I slammed the brakes and jumped out of the car, running toward the ruins. But after only ten yards, I halted, frozen by the sight before me. The entire castle, once a formidable structure, now lay in ruins.

In the short span of an hour and a half since I last saw it, the majestic castle had vanished, reduced to a sprawling heap of debris. The sight was staggering, its sudden collapse almost incomprehensible. I stood there, enveloped by the dust-laden air, unable to tear my eyes away from the devastation.

Time seemed to stand still as I took in the scene. The sea breeze carried the dust toward me, but I was too stunned to move, too overwhelmed by the enormity of what had happened.

Time seemed to stretch endlessly as I grappled with the reality of the castle's sudden collapse. My thoughts were consumed by Degado's fate. What had become of him beneath the rubble?

Finding the entrance to the passage in that heap of ruins seemed an impossible task. Even if I could locate it, digging through the debris would take days, time that Degado didn't have. The realization filled me with a heavy despair. If only we hadn't argued, if only Degado hadn't been injured, if only I hadn't left the castle—perhaps we could have avoided this catastrophe. Instead, I might have been trapped beneath the mountain with him.

In a grim twist of hope, I wished for Degado to remain in his coma, so he might pass quietly without further suffering. It was a harsh thought, but one that offered a sliver of solace in the face of such overwhelming loss.

I remained there until the first light of dawn, the sun slowly revealing the extent of the destruction. The castle's collapse was so thorough that not a single stone seemed to be in its original place. The sight was a stark testament to the fragility of even the mightiest structures.

After a while, I turned away and headed back to the car, driving back to the town. Along the way, a new resolve took hold. In the town, life continued as if oblivious to my presence. People avoided my gaze, perhaps still unnerved by the events at the castle.

I settled my bill at the inn, gathered Degado's and my meager belongings, and left the town behind. My mind was set on a new course of action: I would return to the cave, no matter what it took.

Though the secret passage was now buried, I recalled the possibility of accessing the cave from the sea. It was a daring plan, but one that might allow me to uncover the truth hidden beneath the waves. Determination fueled my decision, and I was resolved to see it through, to dive into the depths and face whatever secrets lay waiting in the cavern.

More than two weeks later, I returned to the site, opting to approach from the sea this time to avoid passing through the town. Accompanied by two experienced divers, I arrived prepared with a reliable boat and top-notch diving equipment.

From a distance, I used a telescope to survey the landscape, confirming that the castle on the mountaintop had indeed become a mere pile of ruins.

The divers with me were well-acquainted with the coastline's geography, aware of the numerous caves nestled beneath the cliffs. They had explored several but had never ventured into the specific cave I described.

We maneuvered the boat close to the cliff, took a brief respite, and then began our dive. I recalled that the path from Degado Castle to the cave was relatively direct, suggesting that the cave lay almost directly below the castle's original location. With this directional guide, finding the cave seemed feasible.

Yet, the first day yielded little success. We discovered wooden frames, blocks, iron structures, and other remnants scattered on the seabed. After examining these with the divers, we concluded they were remnants from when this area operated as a shipyard.

This suggested that Ves Degado had constructed his enigmatic ships under these very cliffs.

On the second day, we expanded our search, diving deeper and covering more ground. This time, we unearthed more iron artifacts, though heavily rusted and fragmented. Their original forms were nearly indiscernible. However, even if they had been perfectly preserved, their bizarre shapes would still have puzzled us.

These pieces seemed like parts of some mechanical apparatus. Could it be that hundreds of years ago, Ves Degado possessed the knowledge to create machines so advanced that even today, they defy our understanding?

The thought was both fascinating and unsettling, suggesting that Ves Degado's secrets were far more complex than previously imagined. Each discovery hinted at a deeper mystery, fueling my resolve to continue unraveling the enigma that lay beneath the waves.

The two divers and I brought several rusted iron artifacts aboard and began the painstaking process of removing the rust to study them closely. It became clear that these were indeed mechanical components, some with visible gears, but their intended purpose remained elusive. One diver speculated that they might have been advanced tools designed by ingenious technicians at the shipyard, such as pulleys or cranes. While it was a plausible theory, I couldn't help but question it given the complexity of the pieces.

On the third day, we made a significant breakthrough. One of the divers spotted a narrow gap and, after a brief discussion, we all converged at the site, illuminating the opening with powerful underwater lights. The beam revealed two large moray eels retreating deeper into the crevice. The passage appeared long and narrow, and we decided to venture in.

I led the way, the strong light cutting through the water as we navigated past clumps of seaweed and increasingly tall rocks. With a sense of anticipation, I finally emerged from the water into a cave, the same cave I had been searching for.

There was no mistaking it—this was the cave. The divers surfaced beside me, their expressions mirroring my own surprise as they took in the sight of the large iron box. I quickly swam to the big rock, my mind racing with thoughts of Degado.

I knew Degado couldn't have survived, being trapped in the cave for twenty days. While I had initially worried about his fate, now my thoughts turned to the condition of his body. Yet, as I reached the large rock, a shocking sight awaited me.

To my astonishment, Degado was not there. The rock, which I expected to find occupied by his remains, was conspicuously empty. I stood there, bewildered, as questions flooded my mind. Where was Degado's body? What had happened in the intervening days?

The mystery deepened, leaving me with more questions than answers as I stood in the eerie silence of the cave.

The large iron box remained on the big rock, but Degado was nowhere to be found. The last time I was here, I had positioned his unconscious body close to the box, but now he had vanished.

It was possible that he had regained consciousness and perhaps even summoned the strength to climb up. But once he realized that the way out was obstructed, what would he have done? The thought was too distressing to dwell on.

The two divers joined me on the rock, aware that I was searching for someone. "It looks like your companion is gone," one of them remarked.

I sighed deeply, feeling the weight of the situation. "Where could he have gone? The exit is blocked!"

One diver speculated, "Maybe he tried to swim out but didn't make it."

I shook my head. "That's impossible. He didn't have any diving equipment and wouldn't have survived in the water."

Gesturing toward the iron box, I explained, "We argued inside the box, and he fell from the edge. He was unconscious when I left." Out of curiosity, the divers stacked up, one climbing onto the other's shoulders to peer into the box. The one on top turned back to me. "It's completely empty, there's nothing inside."

His words left me stunned. "There should be something in there—some inexplicable things!"

He turned back, shining his light inside the box, then looked at me with a bemused expression. "Come see for yourself."

I climbed up, using his shoulders for support, and when I peered inside, I was equally astonished.

The iron box was indeed empty, devoid of anything at all.

The realization hit me like a wave. Finding Degado missing had been shocking enough, but at least there was a possibility he had moved or succumbed to the sea. But the contents of the iron box had vanished without a trace.

There had been numerous items in there—another small iron box, scraps of paper, a basin. Yet now, there was nothing. The mystery deepened, leaving me grappling with confusion and a sense of eerie unease.

What could have happened to Degado, and where had all those items gone? The unanswered questions loomed large in the silence of the cave.

The realization that Degado was missing left me stunned, but his absence seemed somewhat plausible if he had woken up and met his fate in the water. Yet, the disappearance of the items from the iron box was another matter entirely. The box had contained numerous objects: another small iron box, scraps of paper, a basin, and various rusted items like knives, pliers, and what seemed to be surgical tools, plus a large rack. Even if Degado had left, it was inconceivable that he would take all those things with him, particularly given their size and nature.

My body trembled with an unsettling mix of fear and confusion. The divers, sensing the eerie atmosphere, spoke up, "There's nothing here. Let's go. It's too strange."

They were hired for this dive, and I couldn't blame them for wanting to leave. I, too, felt the pull to leave, yet the mystery gnawed at me, leaving me reluctant to abandon the search.

As I prepared to depart, the light in my hand shifted, catching on something unexpected. A patch of rust on the iron box's inner wall flaked away, revealing a line of words. I quickly focused the light on it, calling out, "Wait, I've found something!"

The words etched into the metal were simple but chilling: "He took me away."

The message appeared to have been carved with a knife, the letters unmistakably in English. I recognized the handwriting immediately as belonging to Degado. A shiver ran down my spine as I processed the implications of that message.

Degado had left a final note, cryptic and unsettling. "He took me away." Who was "he"? What did Degado mean by this message? The obscurity of the note added layers to the mystery, suggesting that whatever happened here was far from ordinary.

The divers and I exchanged glances, their expressions mirroring my own bewilderment. The discovery opened a new dimension to the puzzle, one that I couldn't ignore.

A chill ran down my spine as I pondered the message: "He took me away." Its meaning was straightforward— someone had taken Degado from the cave. But the identity of this mysterious "he" was elusive and troubling.

The divers, still on the big rock, were curious about my discovery, asking repeatedly, "What did you find?" Yet, I couldn't bring myself to respond. The revelation had left me speechless, unable to articulate my thoughts or the creeping unease that gripped me.

Without further delay, I descended from the diver's shoulder and simply said, "We should go." The divers were visibly relieved to hear this, quickly securing their oxygen cylinders before diving back into the water. I didn't linger either, soon following them into the narrow passage and swimming back to the boat.

Once aboard, I sat in a daze, overwhelmed by the strangeness of the situation. My life had been filled with bizarre experiences, but none as convoluted as this. From the moment Captain Moore had first involved me, each discovery seemed to raise more questions than answers, spiraling into a complex web of uncertainty.

As the divers steered the boat away, I remained on the deck, eyes closed, replaying the sequence of events in my mind. The puzzle pieces were scattered and incomplete, and despite my efforts, I couldn't form a coherent picture.

It seemed everything hinged on Ves Degado, the enigmatic figure at the heart of the mystery.

Who was the "he" in Degado's message? What had truly happened in that cave?

As I mulled over the mystery, a wild thought struck me: could Degado have been taken by his ancestor, Ves Degado? The idea seemed absurd. The notion that Ves

Degado could still be alive, and not only alive but active and free to do as he pleased, was beyond belief.

Even if this outlandish theory were true, what could I possibly do about it? Ves Degado was a ghost of the past, and truthfully, I had no desire to encounter him. The whole affair, which had spiraled from Captain Moore's initial involvement, had reached a level of complexity I hadn't anticipated.

I resolved to put it behind me, though moving on proved to be a challenge.

Some time later, at a social gathering, I stumbled upon a conversation with a renowned marine biologist about the concept of mermaids. His response was dismissive, "Mermaids? You've been reading too many fantasy novels!"

His casual dismissal irked me. I valued a serious approach to questions, especially from those in scientific fields. Frustrated, I retorted, "I don't just read them—I write fantasy novels!"

The biologist paused, then apologized. "I assumed you were joking. From a fantasy perspective, mermaids are fascinating, but scientifically, they don't exist."

I challenged him, "Why not? The ocean is home to countless bizarre creatures. Mammals like whales thrive there; why not mermaids?"

He pondered my question, explaining, "If there were a creature half-human, half-fish, it would still be a fish, not a human. It wouldn't possess human-like intelligence and live similarly in the ocean."

He added confidently, "That scenario is impossible."

I countered, "Marine life can be intelligent. Dolphins are as smart as gorillas. Could mermaids exist—or have existed?"

The biologist shrugged. "Without evidence—like a specimen or fossil—we can't confirm any creature's existence. We can't just imagine fantastical beings like eight-headed monsters."

His pragmatic view was disheartening, but I understood his point. Science required tangible evidence, not speculation.

The marine biologist's skepticism was palpable, but I couldn't help but sigh when faced with his doubt. When he noticed my reaction, he asked, "What's the matter?"

Instead of explaining, I requested a piece of paper and sketched the two skeletons I had seen in the small iron boxes in the cave. Despite my lack of artistic skill, the memory was vivid enough for me to capture their likeness accurately.

After finishing, I handed the paper to the biologist. "Whether you believe it or not, I've seen two skeletons like these. What do you make of them?"

He studied the drawing intently, his expression shifting to one of serious contemplation. After a long pause, he asked, "Where are these skeletons?"

I gave a bitter smile. "I saw them, but they fell into the sea. When I returned to find them, they were gone. I know they hold immense biological significance, but they're lost."

Our conversation had drawn the attention of others nearby. One person interjected with a dismissive comment, "Ha, it's like someone claiming they've seen aliens!"

I turned to the speaker, irritated by the interruption. "I'm not discussing this with you. Please keep your superficial opinions to yourself!"

My sharp response left the person embarrassed, but I didn't care. I was seeking expert insight, not idle chatter from skeptics who hadn't seen what I had.

Returning my focus to the biologist, I watched as he continued to examine the drawing. Finally, he spoke slowly, "If the skeletons you saw truly resembled this, then they might be mermaids. But that seems impossible. No one else has ever documented such a creature."

His words were a mix of acknowledgment and disbelief. While he entertained the possibility based on my account, the absence of corroborating evidence left him doubtful.

The conversation left me with a mix of frustration and curiosity. While I still lacked definitive answers, the biologist's tentative admission that my sighting could suggest something extraordinary was a small validation of my experience. Yet, the mystery remained unresolved, a tantalizing enigma that continued to linger in my thoughts.

I offered a bitter smile as I posed a thought-provoking question to the biologist, "If I suggest there's a person, entirely human, who can live in the sea, you'd believe it even less, wouldn't you?"

I knew this was a challenging question for a biologist, and his chuckle in response was expected. After a hearty laugh, he patted my shoulder and suggested we drop the topic. But my curiosity wouldn't let me stop.

"Wait," I insisted. "Let's hypothesize that mermaids exist—beings like humans living in the sea. Assuming this, I have another question."

The biologist regarded me with curiosity as I continued, "Could a normal person learn to live in the ocean from mermaids?"

He shook his head, explaining, "No, the key to biological life is oxygen. Humans breathe air directly, whereas fish extract oxygen from water. Their respiratory systems are fundamentally different and can't be changed, unless—"

I leaned in, eager for the rest. "Unless what?" I pressed.

With a smile, he replied, "Unless the respiratory system of a mermaid—assuming mermaids exist—were transplanted into a human, and the human's body accepted these organs without rejection. Then, that person could naturally live underwater."

His hypothetical scenario left me in a thoughtful daze. Perhaps I lingered in that state for too long, or maybe the biologist had tired of my seemingly nonsensical inquiries. When I snapped back to reality, I found myself alone on the sofa.

In that moment of solitude, my mind was a whirlwind of confusion. I could only speculate, but one thing felt certain: the existence of mermaids.

From a fantasy perspective, as the biologist suggested, the entire series of events could be interpreted as follows:

1) Ves Degado captured not one, but two mermaids—ethereal beings of the deep whose existence defies the boundaries of myth and reality.

2) In the shadowy recesses of his hidden shipyard, Ves Degado constructed three enigmatic vessels. The design of these ships was extraordinary, rumored to contain mechanical devices allowing them to navigate ocean depths like modern submarines, rising and falling with uncanny grace.

3) Among his audacious experiments, Ves Degado transplanted the mermaids' respiratory organs. The surgical tools discovered in the large iron box—rusty knives and peculiar implements—hint at procedures that blur the line between science and the arcane.

4) Astonishingly, Ves Degado is still alive today. How he defies the march of time remains a mystery. Does the ocean's embrace grant its denizens a prolonged existence, or has Ves Degado unearthed secrets known only to the depths?

5) There are tales of ghostly vessels that drift silently across the waves. Moore and I have encountered this apparition, and it must be none other than Ves Degado himself, still navigating the seas with his otherworldly knowledge.

6) The enigma deepens as Ves Degado spirited away his own descendants. Did he bestow upon them the ability to dwell beneath the waves? Or perhaps he has once again sought the mermaids, repeating his ancient rites to extend his legacy?

From the depths of my imagination, I've woven together this outline—a tapestry of fantasy and speculation.

Yet, the true answers lie hidden beneath the waves, awaiting discovery.

Only by finding Ves Degado can we hope to unravel the full story. But the ocean's vastness is daunting. It stretches endlessly, a blue expanse that conceals its secrets well. I recall tales from World War II, where the U.S. Air Force spent an entire year scouring the seas for a single Japanese battleship.

If there are those with the courage and curiosity to embark on such a quest to find Ves Degado, I will not stand in their way. Let them venture into the unknown, guided by whispers of legend and the allure of the sea's hidden mysteries.

As for me, my journey ends here. The ocean has claimed enough of my spirit, and I will not return to its depths in search of answers that may never be found.

Epilogue

The tale has reached its conclusion.

There are those who claim that every story, regardless of its coherence, should find closure within its own world. So why does this one seem to linger without a definitive beginning or end?

In truth, this story is not without its own framework. It began on the fateful day Captain Moore came to me, setting events into motion, and it reaches its enigmatic conclusion with the mysterious disappearance of Degado.

While the narrative may not follow a traditional path, it is no less complete. It weaves through the realms of myth and reality, leaving threads of mystery that invite contemplation. The questions it raises linger in the mind, whispering of possibilities that extend beyond the written words.

In the end, perhaps that is the true essence of this story—an invitation to ponder the unknown, to embrace the allure of the unsolved, and to find meaning in the journey itself, rather than in a neatly tied bow of resolution.

No one truly knows where Degado went. The only clue lies in the haunting words he carved into the rust of the big iron box: "He took me away." This cryptic message suggests he was taken by someone, and the only person capable of such a feat seems to be Ves Degado.

For those who find the tale of Ves Degado hard to accept, another possibility comes to light. In his final, delirious moments, Degado might have conjured a vision of Ves Degado standing before him. In his confusion, he may have "followed" this phantom into the depths of the sea.

If this is indeed what transpired, then Degado's end was a tragic one—a misfortune that befell him like countless other unfortunate events that pepper the human experience.

Alas, the world is filled with such misfortunes! They come in many forms, weaving a narrative of loss and mystery that challenges our understanding and reminds us of the fragility of life.